'Are you o
Helen asked

Suddenly realising that she wanted him to, desperately, because for no very good reason that she could think of it had suddenly become very important to her to be here, in this village, working in this surgery.

No *good* reason. Just a very bad one, she realised, and he was standing in front of her. All that latent masculinity, the coiled energy, the extraordinarily lively intelligence in those astonishing blue eyes—it all added up to a very potent package, and she had a terrible urge to unwrap it.

Foolish, silly girl. Run! Get out!

'Sure, I'm offering you the job. I'd be an idiot not to. I just hope you'll take it.'

'Great. Thank you. I'll take it,' she said, and found her hand wrapped in his, their eyes locked.

Heat shot through her, and any doubts she'd had about her sanity were instantly dispelled. She was definitely, certifiably, off her trolley.

Caroline Anderson has the mind of a butterfly. She's been a nurse, a secretary, a teacher, run her own soft-furnishing business and now she's settled on writing. She says, 'I was looking for that elusive something. I finally realised it was variety, and now I have it in abundance. Every book brings new horizons and new friends, and in between books I have learned to be a juggler. My teacher husband John and I have two beautiful and talented daughters, Sarah and Hannah, umpteen pets and several acres of Suffolk that nature tries to reclaim every time we turn our backs!' Caroline also writes for the Mills & Boon Tender Romance® series.

A VERY SINGLE WOMAN

BY

CAROLINE ANDERSON

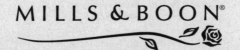

MILLS & BOON®

First published in Great Britain 2002
Harlequin Mills & Boon Limited,
Eton House, 18-24 Paradise Road, Richmond, Surrey TW9 1SR

© Caroline Anderson 2002

ISBN 0 263 83070 5

Set in Times Roman 10½ on 12½ pt.
03-0602-45519

Printed and bound in Spain
by Litografía Rosés, S.A., Barcelona

CHAPTER ONE

SHE was late, of course. It was absolutely the last thing Nick needed, at the end of a busy week and with the locum off sick and his partner on compassionate leave.

And Sam would be waiting at his grandparents', champing at the bit because Nick had promised to build him the tree-house this weekend and they were going to start this evening. Correction, they *had* been going to start this evening, but he couldn't leave until his interviewee arrived, and she'd phoned over an hour ago and said she was on her way.

If she hadn't been such a perfect fit for their requirements, he would have told her she'd blown it by failing to arrive on time, but she was too good to miss.

He looked at the application form again, studying it grimly for weaknesses. There were none. Well, none that he could see. He turned over the page and read her CV, and was reluctantly impressed.

It seemed that the thirty-four-year-old Dr Helen Moore was clever, had wide experience in the areas that mattered and, even more unbelievably, apparently wanted to come to their quiet little neck of the woods and take the part-time job they'd advertised in a fit of blind optimism.

Why? Why would anybody in their right mind

want to come to this sleepy corner of Suffolk? Never mind someone as well qualified as Helen Moore.

Except, of course, that she wasn't here yet. She'd probably driven through the village and headed for home, like any sensible person would.

A car pulled up in front of the surgery, and a tall, leggy blonde unravelled herself from the seat, threw her long hair back away from her face and shook it out, then after a momentary hesitation smoothed her skirt, straightened her shoulders and headed for the door.

Her legs were bare in deference to the heat, long and tanned and sleek beneath the demure knee-length hem of her pale linen dress—and utterly gorgeous. Something slow and deep and elemental stirred inside him, fanning the last ember of a long-forgotten fire.

'Behave yourself, for God's sake,' he growled at himself, and went out into Reception to greet her. 'Dr Moore?'

'That's right. I'm so sorry I'm late.'

'Don't worry,' he said quickly. He would have forgiven her anything at that moment, he realised, and gave himself a swift mental shake.

He held out his hand, and hers vanished inside it, smooth and cool and firm, and the glimmering ember turned into a conflagration and threatened to engulf him. He dropped her hand like a hot potato and waved at the door of his room, struggling for air and the simple elements of polite conversation that had eluded him completely. 'I'm Nick Lancaster. Come on in, Dr Moore.'

'Please, call me Helen,' she said, and her voice was

like cream, rich and deep and mellow, with a tinge of huskiness that scraped over his nerve-endings and left him gasping for breath.

She can't be this beautiful *and* clever, he told himself frantically. The CV must be a lie. And why isn't she married?

He nearly asked her, nearly blurted out the question, but he bit the inside of his cheek and dropped into his chair, picking up a pencil and fiddling with it under the edge of the desk. 'So, you had car trouble?'

She smiled apologetically. 'Yes. I'm so sorry. It was really stupid—I had a fractured fuel line and ran out of petrol. I suppose I was lucky it didn't catch fire, really. I might have gone up in flames.'

Join the club, Nick thought grimly. He dragged his eyes from the modest but hinting neck of the dress and the tempting swell of her breasts beneath. 'Never mind, you're here now,' he said, his voice sounding rusty and a little gruff. He cleared his throat. 'Ah— um, I see you're working in Suffolk already, so why the move, and why the change to part time?'

She sat up a little straighter, her jaw firming. 'Is there a law against it?' she asked, and he blinked.

'Of course not,' he said hastily, conjuring up a smile. 'It just seems—well, a little unlikely. I wondered if there was a reason, apart from the obvious one of not wanting to work all the hours that God sends and then some.'

She nodded, a slight tilt of her head in acknowledgement. 'There is a reason, of course. I want to work part time so I can look after my child,' she said quietly. Guardedly?

That threw him. There had been no mention of a child. 'What about your partner, if you have one?' he asked, treading on thin ice. He wasn't allowed to ask these sorts of questions, but Nick didn't care very much about what he was and wasn't allowed to do— not if it got in his way. 'Will he move, too,' he went on, 'or will you commute? It's quite a long way.'

'I'm alone,' she said, and the pencil disintegrated, spraying his stone-coloured chinos with bits of lead and wood. He dropped the shattered remnants into the bin and swept the splinters off his legs surreptitiously, leaving a scatter of grey marks on the pale fabric. Damn. He pulled himself together and wondered if that was laughter he could see in the depths of her eyes—the pale grey-green eyes that so exactly matched her dress.

'Snap,' he said appropriately, and nearly groaned aloud. What an idiot. 'I'm a single parent, too,' he offered. 'I've got a son, Sam. He's eight. What about you? Have you got a boy or a girl?'

She hesitated momentarily, then seemed to stiffen her spine. 'I don't know yet.'

Of their own volition his eyes shot to her board-flat abdomen in the elegant, understated dress, and he felt one eyebrow crawl up into his hairline. He dragged it down and sat forwards, propping his elbows on the desk and staring down at the CV for inspiration. There was none to be found, so he looked her in the eye again and struck another blow for political incorrectness.

'Pardon me for stating the obvious, but you don't look very pregnant,' he commented.

'Well, no, I wouldn't,' she said enigmatically.

Great. It was all to come—morning sickness, days off for antenatal care—maternity leave, for heaven's sake! He heaved a sigh and stabbed his fingers through his hair, rumpling it still further.

'I'm sorry, I know I'm not allowed to ask these questions, but you have to see where I'm coming from. We need a person now—part time, granted, but regular, someone who'll come in every day and do the job required of them, not disappear on maternity leave.'

'Oh, I won't be. Taking maternity leave, that is. I'm not pregnant.'

'But you've got a child—or you're going to have one, of indeterminate sex? That implies pregnancy— so if you aren't pregnant now, presumably you intend to be so at some point in the near future?'

She stood up, her eyes firing pale green sparks. 'Dr Lancaster, you're right, you're totally out of order, but for your information I'm actually intending to adopt—although since you clearly aren't interested in having another single parent in the practice, I won't take any more of your time—'

'No! Dr Moore—Helen—wait!'

He all but vaulted over the edge of the desk and took her arm, preventing her escape. 'I'm sorry, I didn't mean to— Oh, hell.' He stabbed a hand through his hair again and met her eyes with a crooked and repentant smile. 'Can we start again?'

'What, now you know all the personal things you

aren't supposed to ask about?' Her voice was chilling, and she looked down pointedly at his hand on her arm.

He dropped it and stepped back, carefully positioning himself so he was between her and the door.

'I'm sorry,' he said again, his smile slipping. 'I was way out of line, but you know what it's like in a small practice. There's precious little room to manoeuvre. It's hard enough making allowances for me and my son, and I have my parents here in the village to help me look after him. If you move here alone, without a support system, naturally it'll be harder when things go wrong, but I'm sure we can work round it if necessary. Nothing's insurmountable.' He gave her his coaxing, little-boy grin again. 'Please, let's talk it through, let me show you the practice, then you can decide.'

She hesitated a moment, her even, translucent white teeth nibbling thoughtfully at the corner of her lip, and then she sighed and sat down again, and he felt the breath rush out of him, leaving him weak. He sat down in a hurry before his legs deserted him, and his mouth tilted up at one corner in relief.

'Thank you,' he said, and as she looked up at him across the desk their eyes met, and he felt the shock of it right down to his toes.

It was like being struck by lightning, Helen thought in a daze. Cobalt blue lightning, spearing through her and pinning her to the chair. What a smile—even if he did ask the damnedest questions!

She dragged her eyes from his and reminded herself that she wasn't interested. She didn't do relation-ships—and most particularly not with potential col-leagues with eyes like a Mediterranean night sky and a smile that could melt the soles of her shoes.

'So,' he was saying, 'you're planning to adopt a child, and you want a part-time job. If I might say so, that's very brave of you.'

'Taking on a child alone? Lots of people do it.'

'Lots of people have to,' he pointed out, his eyes clouding slightly. 'Most of us don't do it out of choice.'

She wondered what had happened, but she wasn't going to give him the satisfaction of asking, or open the floodgates to any further penetrating questions. 'I don't have a choice either,' she said flatly, and won-dered if the bleak tone in her voice was audible only to her own ears, or if Dr Lancaster would hear it and pick up on it.

'About the practice,' she said, dragging the inter-view firmly back into line, and for the next few minutes the talk was all of patient numbers and targets and clinics and frustrations and the limitations of the job, and she found herself totally in agreement with him. If only he would stick to business and not pry, she was sure they'd get on fine.

If.

She didn't think there was a lot of chance. Dr Nick Lancaster, with his laughing blue eyes and evident passion for his job, wasn't a person to stick to the rules or stay behind lines drawn in the sand. Still, it was a lovely part of Suffolk, not too far from her mother and sister, and it seemed a safe little place to bring up a child.

And, with a part-time job instead of full time, she'd be more likely to be given the go-ahead to adopt.

'Have a look round,' he said, shooting back his chair and getting to his feet. He held the door for her, and as she passed through it she was suddenly utterly aware of him, of the very essence of him—the sheer power of his body, the faint scent of soap and warm skin, the way his shirt moved over the lean, muscled contours of his shoulders, the neat hips and long legs encased in trousers so well cut they merely hinted at all that masculinity.

Stupid. She wasn't interested. She didn't do relationships with colleagues—with anyone, she corrected herself. Not now. Not any more. Too messy, too heartbreaking, too dangerous, especially if there was a child involved. She particularly didn't do relationships where there was a child involved.

She followed him out into the surgery, and they went into all the other consulting rooms, the clinics and the office, pausing to collect a plastic cup of chilled water from the dispenser before moving on. The huge plastic bottle gurgled to a halt, and he sighed and changed it, hefting the new bottle into place effortlessly.

Helen sipped her cool, refreshing water and tried not to look, not to notice the ripple of muscle under his shirt, but her eyes had decided not to obey her today and it was a fruitless task. Perhaps she should just dump the cold water on her head to settle herself down.

He turned to her with a grin. 'Now I won't be in trouble with the reception staff tomorrow morning,' he said, as if it was likely that anyone with that smile would be in trouble with anyone for long.

'God forbid,' she murmured, and he chuckled, propping up the counter behind him and eyeing her thoughtfully.

'So, Dr Moore, what's the verdict? Can you forgive me my intrusive questioning and work with us?'

'Are you offering me the job?' she asked levelly, suddenly realising that she wanted him to, desperately, because for no very good reason that she could think of it had suddenly become very important to her to be here, in this village, working in this surgery.

No *good* reason. Just a very bad one, she realised, and he was standing in front of her, about as bad as they came, looking rumpled and sexy and as safe as a rumbling volcano. All that latent masculinity, the coiled energy, the extraordinarily lively intelligence in those astonishing blue eyes—it all added up to a very potent and dangerous package, and she had a terrible urge to unwrap it.

Foolish, silly girl. Run! her mind screamed. Get out!

'I think we could work together,' he said, serious now. 'We're looking for a woman to achieve a little balance in the practice. Some of our female patients prefer to see another woman, and many of the children are happier. It makes sense. You're the only woman that's applied who we'd consider, and you're more than adequate for the job, as you must be aware.' He shrugged. 'Sure, I'm offering you the job. I'd be an idiot not to. I just hope you'll take it.'

'What about my child-care arrangements?' she asked, reminding him that she wasn't, in fact, the perfect candidate.

He shrugged again. 'It'll work if you want it to. I have no doubt there'll be hiccups, but we can deal with that. We're flexible. It cuts both ways. There are times when I can't be one hundred per cent reliable either. That's OK. We're human.'

Very human. Human and male and dangerous. Run!

'Great. Thank you. I'll take it,' she said, and found her hand wrapped in his, their eyes locked.

Heat shot through her, and any doubts she'd had about her sanity were instantly dispelled. She was definitely, certifiably off her trolley.

Nick couldn't believe it. She'd accepted—even after his somewhat unorthodox interview and the litigation he'd nearly got himself involved in. He glanced at his watch and tunnelled his hand through his hair again.

'Look, I have to go and pick up my son, because my parents are going out to the theatre tonight, but if you aren't in a hurry we could pick up a take-away and go back to my place and finalise a few details.'

He held his breath while she vacillated. Those pretty little teeth nibbled her lip again in the unconscious gesture that sent blood rushing through his veins with unseemly haste. He scrubbed a hand over his chin, aware of the stubble and the slight salty stickiness at the end of a long, scorching June day.

What he really wanted was to go home and get into a shower, pour himself a gin and tonic and sit down in the garden with his feet up. Instead, he was either going to end up taking Helen home for a Chinese or grovelling about in the woodpile with Sam and building a tree-house.

Guilt and need gnawed at him in equal parts, but he was used to that. Used to both, although the need thing usually didn't trouble him too much during the day. It normally waited for the small hours of the night, or if he was watching a romantic film late in the evening after Sam was in bed.

It had been years since he'd even noticed a real woman, but he'd noticed this one, and he suddenly regretted issuing the invitation. He had to work with her, had to treat her as a colleague and not embarrass himself in front of her every time he saw her.

And taking her back to his house so she could imprint herself on it in a series of tormenting images was about the most foolish thing he could think of doing. Maybe she'd say no.

'That would be lovely, actually,' she said in her soft, well-modulated voice that played hell with his nerves. 'I missed lunch and I'm ravenous.' Her smile was spontaneous and open and landed right on target. He nearly groaned aloud.

'What do you fancy—Chinese? Indian? We've got both in the village, miraculously.'

'Chinese, if that's OK?'

'Fine. Any preference for dishes?' he asked, reaching for the phone.

She shook her head, and he stabbed in the number

of the take-away and ordered a set meal for three and extra rice.

'Great, let's go. Do you want to follow me?'

She nodded. 'Fine.'

He shut the window in his room, checked the surgery once more and locked up, setting the alarm on the way out. He phoned his parents on the way there, and they were waiting on the kerb with Sam as he pulled up.

'Hi, Sam,' he said with a smile, but his son just looked at him.

'You're late,' he said accusingly. 'We were going to build my tree-house.'

'I know. I'm sorry. The lady who was coming for interview was held up. In fact, she's coming back to the house with us because she's hungry, and we're going to get a Chinese. How does that sound?'

'Horrible. I wanted to do the tree-house—and anyway, Granny gave me supper,' he said flatly, and Nick's heart sank.

'I'm sure you can manage a bit of lemon chicken,' he coaxed, but Sam just shrugged.

'We'll do the tree-house tomorrow, after my morning surgery, I promise.'

Sam just made a disparaging noise and sat back, turning his head away, and Nick left him to it. He'd come round. He usually did. Nick pulled up outside the take-away and ran in, grabbed the over-large order and ran back to the car, throwing Helen a smile.

She smiled back, and his body slammed into overdrive again. Hell, he'd have to stop doing this. He was going to embarrass himself—and her, and anybody else around. And just then the anybody in question happened to be his son! It was totally inappropriate, he told himself. Totally.

Except, of course, that she was single, and for some reason she was going to adopt a child. Why? She was beautiful, clever, she had attitude—maybe too much attitude. Maybe she couldn't keep a man because she was just too prickly, but that didn't figure. Her references had emphasised her people skills and her good relationships with her colleagues.

So why was someone like that alone? It was wrong. She shouldn't be, any more than he should, and there was no reason on God's earth why he shouldn't react to her. He found himself wondering if she had fertility problems and if she was alone because of that.

What a wicked shame. All that beauty and intelligence should be passed on to the next generation, not locked up inside her and allowed to go to waste.

'It's none of your business,' he told himself fiercely.

'I didn't say a word!' Sam protested, and he realised he'd spoken out loud. Oh, hell. What else had he said?

'Sorry, son, just a bit distracted. Ignore me.'

'Only if you do my tree-house.'

'Tomorrow,' he vowed, and wondered if it really would happen or if yet again something would get in the way.

Oh, Sue, he thought helplessly, why? Life's just so damned complicated without you.

He turned onto the drive and cut the engine, and

Helen's car glided to a halt beside him. Sam was out and off, and he called him back.

'Sam! Come and meet Dr Moore.'

He turned, defiance etched in every inch of his little body, and walked back to his father's side.

What a beautiful child, Helen thought with a pang of envy, and got out of the car. Beautiful and furious. She dredged up a smile. 'Hi. You must be Sam. I'm Helen. I'm really sorry I've made your father late. I understand you were going to build a tree-house together and I've got in the way. I'm so sorry.'

He scuffed his toe in the gravel and shrugged.

''S' all right. Doesn't matter. It always happens.'

Beside him Nick shrugged helplessly, a sad smile in his eyes, and Helen's soft heart went out to him. She hadn't asked about his wife—personal questions weren't in her repertoire. She didn't invite intrusion into her life, and so she didn't intrude into others', but now she wished she had, because they were obviously still hurting from whatever had happened to them, and she didn't want to put her foot in it.

Still, she didn't know, so she'd just have to work her way round it. She focused her attention on the house instead, and instantly found herself fascinated and enraptured. Built in soft old red bricks, it was curious and interesting, long and low, with a strange round blip on the end.

'What an amazing house,' she said, following Nick in through the broad double door into the entrance hall.

'It used to be a windmill, hence the name. It's

called the Old Post Mill. This bit was the grain store. Come on through to the kitchen, I'll find some plates.'

Helen followed him, conscious all the way of the baleful, resentful look she was getting from his son, but she ignored him. There was nothing she could say that would make it better, and he'd get over it in time. Anyway, it wasn't her problem, it was Nick's.

Besides, she had other things to think about—like Nick's fabulous _kitchen_. It was wonderful, oddly enough a real cook's kitchen, clean and functional but obviously busy, the walls lined with solid pale oak units, the worktops black granite, often-used utensils hung on racks in easy reach. It was just the sort of kitchen she'd always wanted but had never been able to afford, or owned a house worthy of it, and she sighed softly. Sam hitched himself up onto a tall stool and glowered at her across the breakfast bar.

She tried a smile, but his eyes just slid away, so she focused her attention on his father. That was a mistake. His movements were smooth, efficient, and spoke of a body well honed by exercise. Her mind ran off all on its own, and she dragged back forcibly.

'Is there anything I can do to help?' she asked, needing something concrete to do to occupy her mind.

'I think I can probably manage to unwrap a Chinese,' he said with a wry grin. 'You could find us a drink, though. What do you fancy? Have a look in the fridge.'

The fridge was astonishing—one of those amazing American contraptions with a crushed-ice dispenser in the freezer door. She had a look inside the other door. There was a bewildering array of bottles in the door rack, white wine, fizzy drinks, mineral water—too much choice.

'Any preference?' she asked a little helplessly.

He shot her a crooked a grin. 'Personally, I fancy iced water—gallons of it. Sam probably wants something fizzy. What do you fancy, son?'

Sam shrugged awkwardly. 'I dunno. Water.'

His father arched an expressive brow, and Sam's mouth turned even further down at the corners. 'Please,' he said ungraciously, and Helen had to suppress a smile.

'I guess that's three waters, then,' she said brightly. 'Where do I find the glasses?'

Nick pointed at the cupboard, and carried on opening packets. She sniffed appreciatively. 'Smells good.'

'Hopefully it'll taste good. I hope you're hungry. I seem to have ordered rather a lot and Sam tells me he's eaten.'

Right on cue, her tummy rumbled, and he gave a low chuckle. 'I guess that's a yes, then.' He smiled, and she smiled back, unable to resist his good nature.

She gave an inward sigh. She wished Sam had as little trouble resisting her good nature.

'Are you all right in here or do you want to eat in the dining-room?'

'Here's fine. It's a lovely kitchen, I'm jealous.'

'Tough, it's mine. Sam, go and wash your hands.'

Sam slid off the stool and stomped out of the room, and Nick sighed and rammed a hand through his hair. 'Sorry about that,' he said softly. 'I end up disappointing him all the time, because things get in the way, but it can't be helped. Life's a steep learning curve for kids with single parents. You really want to think very carefully about it before you embark on it.'

'I have,' she said quietly. 'Don't worry, I am aware of just how difficult it can be. My mother brought me up on her own, so I know just how steep that learning curve really is.'

She was conscious of his thoughtful look and wondered if he'd follow up on it, but he didn't, not really. At least, he didn't ask any penetrating and awkward questions, merely said, 'Just bear it in mind. Now, come on, dig in. I'm not eating the rest of this for breakfast.'

'Shouldn't we wait for Sam?' she asked, still concerned for his son, but he shook his head.

'He'll come back when he's ready.'

He handed her a spoon, and she helped herself to the various dishes from the little metal cartons. She didn't even give a thought to the calories. She was far too hungry to care. Nick didn't seem to be counting calories either. He piled his plate, speared a king prawn and eyed her over the top of it. 'I haven't yet asked you when you'll be able to start work.'

She paused, the forkful of rice hovering in front of her mouth. 'Any time,' she said. 'I'm on holiday as from today, but I need to arrange accommodation and move nearer, obviously.'

'Do you have a house to sell?' he asked.

She shook her head. 'No. My buyer was in a hurry to complete, so I've already moved out. I'm in a bed and breakfast at the moment, for my sins. I thought it was better to be ready to go than to get stuck in an endless chain.'

'What sort of thing are you looking for?'

She shrugged. 'I don't know. Somewhere nice to bring up a child. I don't mind doing a bit of work, I quite enjoy it. Nothing too expensive, though. I don't want a big mortgage, not on a part-time job.'

'I wonder,' he said thoughtfully. 'I had a patient—she died a couple of months ago. Her cottage is nice—it's only tiny, and it certainly needs a bit of work, but with a bit of imagination you could see that it would be lovely, and it's got a super garden. I've still got the key, actually—forgot to give it back. The auction's on Monday evening, and I think the guide price is pretty low. Fancy a look?'

'Tonight?' she said. 'Is it far away? Only I have to get back.'

'It's only round the corner, but the easy way is over the fence at the end of the garden. That's why I've got the key. I used to keep an eye on her.'

She shrugged. Why not? She had to live somewhere—and the sudden flicker of interest she felt was nothing to do with the fact that it backed onto Nick's garden. Of course not!

'Sounds good,' she said.

He waved his fork at her. 'Eat up, then. You aren't allowed to see it until you've had at least two plate-fuls.'

She ate. She ate till she thought she'd burst, and then she looked up at him and smiled. 'Is that enough?'

He grinned. 'It'll do for starters.'

She gave Sam's plate a thoughtful look. 'Is he coming back?'

'I don't know. Probably not. He's sulking. He'll get over it. He's had supper anyway, so I'm not worried. He can have some later. Ready to go?'

She looked down at her pencil skirt and high heels. 'Can I get over the fence in these?' she asked, and he grinned.

'I should think so. There's a gate—well, a panel that lifts out of the way. Much more dignified. Your shoes might get a bit muddy, though.'

'They'll clean,' she said, suddenly eager. 'Let's go.'

CHAPTER TWO

As THEY left the kitchen and walked down the hall, Nick could hear the television blaring from Sam's bedroom. He felt a pang of guilt—another one to go with all the others—but there was nothing he could do about it. He stuck his head round the door.

'I'm taking Dr Moore to have a look at Mrs Smith's house. We won't be long.' Sam didn't speak, just ducked his head and ignored him. He sighed inwardly. He couldn't blame the kid, but he'd get his tree-house tomorrow. He'd have to, or Nick's life wouldn't be worth living. The guilt would kill him.

He opened the front door and ushered Helen through it, catching as he did so the delicate scent of her perfume—or was it her skin? Whatever, a wave of heat hit him broadside and he almost groaned aloud.

'At least it's still light,' he said, groping for something intelligent to say. 'And cooler,' he added, thankful for the slight breeze that took the fire out of his skin.

'Only slightly. We spend all winter moaning about the cold, and the moment summer comes we all complain.' She threw him a smile, and for some crazy reason it made his heart jerk against his ribs. This was going to drive him nuts. He strode down the garden, heedless of her struggling behind him in her high heels, and when he reached the fence at the end he yanked the panel out of the way almost viciously.

'Here we are. It's a bit overgrown at the moment, but with the weather we've had everything's been shooting up. Still, the roses seem to love it.'

Helen followed him through the gap and looked around, her eyes taking in the wild tangle of garden. 'It's gorgeous!' she said breathlessly. 'Oh, Nick, it's wonderful! I've always wanted a garden like this.'

'You haven't seen the inside of the cottage yet.' He laughed. 'You might absolutely hate it.'

'It'll have to be dreadful to put me off,' she said with a smile.

He walked up the path, and the drooping lupins brushed against his legs. The garden sorely needed attention, but that wasn't his job. He didn't, in fact, have a reason to be here at all any more now that Mrs Smith was dead, and he probably should have given the key back, but the son seemed quite keen for him to have it, and if he could manage to sell the house he was sure they would all be grateful.

Leave alone his own feelings in the matter. He didn't want to analyse them. He had a feeling that his interest in finding Dr Moore a house quite so close to his own had little to do with settling her quickly into the area and much more to do with having her very much at hand. He pushed the key into the lock, turned it and swung the door open, sniffing as he walked in.

'It smells a bit musty, I'm afraid, but it's been shut up for about three months,' he said apologetically. 'Try not to see it as it is—try and imagine what it

could be like freshly decorated with some decent carpets and curtains.'

He turned to look at her, and caught the dismay on
her face.

'Freshly decorated?' she said with a choked laugh.
'It'll take more than a coat of paint to sort this lot
out.' She looked around her, and as they walked
through the rooms, upstairs and down, he saw her
draw herself up as if to accept the challenge. 'On the
other hand, you're right, it could be lovely, and I can
forgive it anything because of the garden.' She turned
to him and met his eyes. 'You say the auction's on
Monday?'

'That's right—six-thirty.'

'Any idea how much it's going to be?'

'None, I'm afraid—the guide is only that. I can find
out the name of the agent for you, but I doubt if you'd
be able to move into it straight away anyway in its
current condition.' Nick eyed her thoughtfully. 'I
don't suppose there's the slightest chance we could
talk you into sleeping at the practice and starting on
Monday, is there? It's just that, if you're already
available, we could really use you straight away. My
partner's mother's died in a nasty accident, and his
father is deranged with grief, so Lawrence is on compassionate leave. And as if that wasn't enough, the
locum we got in to take up the slack has gone and
got himself chickenpox, so he's out of the picture
now. There's a room at the practice—quite a nice
room that we used to use when we were on duty—
and you'd have use of the kitchen, so you could ac-

tually make it quite homely in the short term.' He gave her his most persuasive smile, and she chuckled.

'Not that you're putting pressure on me or anything like that, of course.'

'Of course not,' he said with a grin. 'Wouldn't dream of it. However, if you would consider it, you'd have our undying gratitude. Trying to find a new locum for the next couple of weeks will be impossible.'

She tipped her head on one side and smiled at him quizzically. 'Your undying gratitude, eh? I wonder what that's worth?'

Nick groaned. 'I've got a horrible feeling I'm going to regret offering you the post,' he said, a thread of laughter in his voice. He looked around them and then back to Helen. 'Have you seen all you want to see? I'd like to get back to Sam.'

'Yes, that's fine. I'd like to talk to the agent as soon as possible—and, yes, I suppose I could start on Monday if you really, really want me to.'

Nick felt a great weight lift off his shoulders. 'Wonderful! You're a star, Helen Moore,' he said with another smile. 'Thank you.'

Helen thought she must be losing it. He only had to smile at her and she was putty in his hands. Still, if she was going to work here she might as well get into it, and it sounded as if Nick really did need her at the moment. If nothing else, maybe it would mean that Sam could have his tree-house.

And maybe she could have her house, this tired, run-down little Victorian cottage with its wonderful rose garden. Always assuming, of course, that she could afford it. Heaven knows what it would fetch at auction—it would just depend on the night, she realised dispiritedly.

She stiffened her spine. She'd have to afford it, she decided. It was so lovely—correction, it would be so lovely—that she couldn't imagine living anywhere else. And, she thought, following Nick through the gap in the fence, there was the added advantage of being so close to him.

She caught herself on that thought. She really must be going crazy. There was no way she needed to think about being close to him, or close to any man. She didn't do that. She was going to have to make a continuous loop of tape and play it to herself all night— I do not need a man. I do not need a man. I do not need a man...

Or want one.

Her body was calling her a liar, all her senses at full alert as she followed him through the scented, dusky garden, but she ignored the clamouring. There was no way that some physical reaction was going to come between her and her carefully mapped-out future. She had a plan, and she was going to stick to it. First, though, she had to move into a house and get it ready for the arrival of a child. That was all that mattered, all she could let herself think about.

And Nick, for all his long, lean legs and sexy grin, was a very long way down her list of priorities.

Helen was so deep in thought as they approached the house that for a moment she was unaware of the pandemonium that was breaking loose at the entrance to the drive. Nick, though, was wide awake and broke into a run. She followed him, to find him crouched down on the edge of the pavement beside an elderly lady, who was clutching her chest and trying desperately to speak.

'Doctor—you've got to help me, Doctor!' She gasped for breath.

'Take your time,' he said calmly, but she was flustered and panicky. The crowd was growing, a slim woman from across the road coming over to kneel down beside him.

'Anything I can do?' she asked, and Nick shook his head.

'It's Peter,' the elderly woman gasped. 'I don't know what's happened to him, but there's blood everywhere and I don't know what to do! You've got to help me!'

'Don't worry Mrs Emanuel, I'll get the car and we'll go straight there.' He turned and looked up at Helen. 'I don't suppose you could keep an eye on Sam, could you? I'll be as quick as I can.'

'You'll need me,' she said in a low voice. 'Mrs Emanuel needs someone to talk to.'

'I'll look after Sam,' the woman from across the road chipped in, and Nick looked up and smiled in relief.

'He's inside. Could you take him home, Linda? That would be great. Thanks. I'll pick him up later.' He stood up and turned to Helen again. 'Stay with her. I'll get the car and tell Sam what's happening. Linda, can you come with me?'

He sprinted back up the drive, disappearing into the house with Linda for a moment before coming out

still at a run. Seconds later his car was there beside
them, and Helen was helping Mrs Emanuel into the
front seat. She dived in behind her, and without cer-
emony Nick shot off up the road towards the
Emanuels' house.

'Oh, hurry, Doctor!' Mrs Emanuel said desperately,
wringing her hands. 'He's going to bleed to death!'

'Where's the blood coming from?' he asked, and
she shook her head.

'I don't know. He's cut himself somewhere in the
workshop. I do wish he wouldn't go out there, I
begged and pleaded with him not to, but now he's on
the warfarin…'

Helen nearly groaned aloud. Warfarin, of all
things—an anti-clotting drug, commonly used after
strokes and heart attacks to prevent their occurrence.
And poor Mrs Emanuel had left her husband bleeding
like a stuck pig. She must be worried sick. Helen leant
forward slightly and put her hand reassuringly on Mrs
Emanuel's shoulder and gave a gentle squeeze. Thin,
wizened, frantic fingers clutched her own, grateful for
the support.

How much longer? Helen thought. They must be
nearly there, Mrs Emanuel had run from her house to
Nick's.

Just as she was just beginning to wonder at the
elderly woman's stamina, Nick screech to a halt outside a neatly kept little bungalow. By the time Helen
had her seat belt off, he was already out of the car
and on his way round to release Mrs Emanuel. Helen
followed them as they both hurried into the house,
through the front door which had been left hanging

open. They found Mr Emanuel collapsed on the floor in the kitchen, blood everywhere, as he weakly tried to staunch the bleeding from his injured hand.

'It's all right, Mr Emanuel,' Nick said reassuringly. 'I'm here now, let me have a look at it.'

As he released the pressure on the wound, the blood spurted across the kitchen and Mrs Emanuel sagged against Helen with a shocked cry. Nick was there instantly, applying pressure in exactly the right place, snapping instructions out to Helen.

'Get me a clean cloth—and phone the ambulance. Tell them we're at 32 Sadlers Way, and tell them to bring plasma expander. He's got an arterial bleed and he's very shocky.'

Helen could see he was shocky; it was obvious from his pallor, the moist glisten of his skin, the slight tremble in his hands. His wife, also, was in shock. Helen put an arm around her and hugged her while she reached for the phone. 'What's the number for the ambulance station?' she asked.

She stabbed in the numbers as he rapped them out, and quickly gave all the details of the casualty. Directions were harder, and she had to relay them from Nick, but finally she was able to put the phone down and reassure them that the ambulance was on its way.

'Oh, thank God,' Mrs Emanuel said fervently. 'Doctor, tell me he's going to be all right.'

'He'll be fine, Doris,' Nick promised. 'Once the ambulance gets here and they get some plasma expander into him to replace lost fluids and get him to hospital so they can stop this bleeding, he'll be fine.

Helen, can you help me? I want to get a line in. At the very least we can get some saline into him here while we wait.'

Helen found a giving set in his bag, and knelt beside him on the blood-streaked floor.

'You'll have to do it, I can't let go of this,' Nick said quietly. 'In the other arm, I think. You might find the vein a bit elusive, he's lost quite a bit of volume.'

She was lucky and got the line in quickly, attached it to the first bag of saline and squeezed it in, then attached another bag and hung it on the front of the kitchen cupboard, while Mrs Emanuel watched worriedly.

'I can't imagine what he thinks he was doing, messing about in that workshop playing with his chisels,' she said with a touch of asperity. She sounded cross, but Helen knew it was just her way of dealing with her worry. People often seemed cross when they were just actually hugely relieved.

'Can't do a damn thing any more without her worrying about me,' Mr Emanuel muttered from his position on the floor. 'Such an old fusspot.' But it was said with a great deal of affection, and Mrs Emanuel began to cry—not noisily, just a soft, quiet sobbing as the tears slid down her wrinkled cheeks.

'You're an old fool, Peter,' she said tearfully, reaching out to hold his hand, the one that Nick didn't have a death grip on. 'Just promise me, promise me you won't do it again. If I hadn't been here, you might have bled to—' She broke off, too overcome to speak, and pressed her fingers to her mouth. Helen pulled up the kitchen chair and pushed her into it, so that she could sit beside her husband, holding his hand and comforting him until the ambulance arrived.

It wasn't long before they heard the sound of the siren, and then Peter was whisked away, plasma expander already being pumped into him by the ambulance crew. Doris was at his side, looking pale but a little more confident now, and as the doors closed behind them and the ambulance drove away Nick turned to Helen on the front path and gave her a cock-eyed grin.

'Sorry to get you working quite so early on in your contract,' he said ruefully, and she returned his smile.

'That's all right—but how come she came to you? I thought you didn't do house calls in the evening?'

'We don't—but what was I suppose to do? Leave him to bleed to death? She knew I'd come.'

'Naturally,' she said with a smile. 'I take it he's a patient?'

Nick nodded. 'Yes—has been for years. He had a stroke two years ago, and he's prone to clotting, hence the warfarin.' He looked at Helen thoughtfully. 'I'm afraid it hasn't done your interview dress a great deal of good,' he added, and Helen looked down at herself and sighed.

'Hmm.'

'You can't possibly go home like that,' he went on. 'At the very least, you need a shower and a change of clothes, and I have no idea what I've got that might fit you. I don't suppose you've got anything with you?'

She shook her head. 'I didn't intend to get covered in blood, oddly enough,' she said with a slight smile.

He ran his eyes assessingly over her, and shrugged. 'If you turn the bottoms up, my jeans might be all right, and I'm sure I can find you a T-shirt or sweat-shirt or something. Come on, let's go back and get washed and changed. It's nearly ten.'

It was, and night had fallen while they'd been in the Emanuels' house. 'I'll make your car all messy,' she said in dismay, but he just laughed.

'No messier than I will, and I'm going to go in it, you can be sure of that. It's one reason I have leather seats—they wipe clean.'

Leather seats? She hadn't even noticed but, then, she'd hardly been concentrating on the interior of his car in the kerfuffle. They went back into the house where a kindly neighbour was cleaning up the mess as well as she could, and packed up Nick's bag before taking their leave.

Moments later they were back at his house, and he picked up the phone, spoke briefly to Linda, the neighbour who'd kindly had Sam for him, and then ushered Helen down the hall. 'Here,' he said, opening a cupboard and thrusting a warm, fluffy towel at her. 'Use the bathroom—I'll dig you out some clothes and leave them by the door. Hopefully they'll fit. What about your dress—is it dry-clean only, or shall I put it in cold water to soak?'

She gave a wry smile. 'I have no idea. I've only just bought it. I'll look at the label in a minute—I won't be long.'

She was, though, because the hot water felt so wonderful she just stood there while it poured down on her and revelled in it. She heard Nick tap on the door and tell her the clothes were there, and reluctantly she shut off the taps, wrapped herself in the lovely soft towel and opened the door.

There was no sign of him, but she could hear another shower running further down the hall. She picked up the clothes—old, worn jeans as soft as butter, and a floppy shirt in a lovely sandwashed fabric that felt wonderful to the touch.

She put her own underwear back on and tugged on the jeans, wondering how they'd fit, but they were fine. Snug on the hips because, of course, he had such a neat, cute bottom… She sighed and dragged herself up short. Forget his bottom, she told herself sternly. Don't think about him wearing the jeans, about the fabric touching his skin, moulding to his shape. You'll go mad.

She fastened the stud and slid up the zip, then pulled a face. The waist was too big, but he'd put a belt there, too, and once she'd put it on and turned the hems up they were fine. The shirt, of course, was huge, but she didn't mind that. She rolled up the cuffs, looked at herself in the mirror and smiled.

Gone was the sophisticated, elegant woman of earlier. This woman looked as if she'd be at home barefoot and puttering around a kitchen—preferably a kitchen like Nick's—which, of course she would.

Part of the time, anyway. She imagined herself in there, children underfoot, and caught her breath.

No! What on earth was she doing? She almost tore the clothes off again, and only the state of her dress prevented her. They're just clothes, she told herself crossly. They don't change you.

Just make you who you really are.

With a growl of disgust she scooped up the dress and yanked open the door, to surprise Nick who was standing outside, one hand poised to knock.

'Oh, you've got them on—they look fine. How are the jeans?'

'Snug on the bottom, loose on the waist,' she said, and something shifted in his eyes.

They tracked down her, but the shirt covered her to mid-thigh and concealed her from his gaze. 'They're a bit long,' he said unnecessarily.

'They would be. I'm five feet eight, you're probably—what? Six two?'

His mouth kicked up in a twisted smile. 'Something like that. Come and have a drink.'

She did, noticing as she followed him that his hair was still wet, the dark brown strands towel-dried and combed for once, not shovelled into place by his fingers. She wondered how long it would last.

Not long. Sam was back by now, perched on a stool in the kitchen, picking at the lemon chicken and complaining it was cold.

'You were invited to join us,' Nick said, shooing the cat off the worktop and scooping the nearly empty cartons into the bin. 'I've put some on a plate for you in the fridge—you can heat it up in the microwave if you're hungry.'

'Is Mr Emanuel all right?' he asked, and Nick nodded.

'Hope so. He cut himself in the workshop on a chisel.'

Sam eyed the bloody dress wadded up in Helen's hand, and pulled a face. 'Gross,' he said, and she grinned.

'Absolutely. I had to borrow your dad's clothes.'

'They're a bit big,' Sam said unnecessarily, and she chuckled.

'I had noticed,' she said drily. 'Still, beggars can't be choosers.'

'Are you a beggar?' Sam said, eyes wide.

Helen nearly laughed aloud. At least he looked as if it was only a remote possibility. 'Not exactly. I'm a doctor.'

'I know that,' Sam said scornfully. The microwave pinged and he took his food out and hitched himself up at the breakfast bar again.

'Mind that, it might be very hot in places,' Nick warned, and slid a glass of water across the counter to him. 'Helen, what can I get you to drink?'

She looked at her watch. It was ten-thirty, and she had an hour's drive ahead of her. 'Coffee, please— nice and strong. I need to stay awake.'

'Don't tell him strong, he makes it like mud, everybody says so,' Sam said through a mouthful of lemon chicken.

She met Nick's laughing, rueful eyes and arched a brow. 'Just normally strong?' she said hopefully.

'Real or instant?'

'Instant's fine. I ought to be getting on.'

'You could stay,' he said, and she had a sudden unheralded vision of herself in his arms.

She felt the heat rising, warming her throat, easing over her cheeks. She cleared her throat and turned away, making a production of sitting on a stool by Sam. 'I don't think so. I've got a lot to do if I'm starting on Monday, but thanks anyway.'

'You could see the room at the practice in the morning,' he suggested, and she was almost tempted, but then she shook her head.

'I'm sure I can imagine it. I'll come back on Sunday afternoon, if that's all right, and get settled in. I may need some time off, of course, in a little while, so I can move up here properly—will that be all right?'

'Fine. Whatever. I'm just so grateful for the help now. I was beginning to wonder what on earth I was going to do for the next few days.'

'Send them all home with their ingrowing toenails and their insomnia because they drink too much tea last thing at night. Most of them don't need to see you, anyway,' she said with her usual blunt humour.

He laughed softly. 'You're so right. If only just the people who were truly sick came to us, we could save the country a fortune and provide a much more efficient service.'

'I'm going to bed,' Sam said, sliding off the stool and heading for the door.

'Night, sport,' Nick said, and Sam raised a hand casually as he walked out. No goodnight kiss, no hug, Helen thought, but maybe he imagined he was too old, or maybe Nick didn't encourage it, or maybe it was because she was there.

She drank her coffee, trying hard not to think about

Nick struggling to bring up a child alone and play the part of both parents. It could be done. Lots of people did it—she was going to do it herself, and make a success of it.

So why, then, was she feeling sorry for this big, gentle man with the laughing eyes and the sexy little bottom and a smile to die for?

She needed to get out of there, to go home to her bed and breakfast so she was up in time to talk to the estate agents tomorrow—and, above all, she needed to be out of his company before she said or did something silly that she'd regret.

She put her mug down, only half-finished, and stood up. 'I must go. I won't be home till midnight as it is,' she told him, and he nodded.

'Drive carefully,' he said, his voice low and soft, almost as if he cared, and she found herself wishing he did, that she could dare to have a man like Nick caring for her.

But she couldn't, and she wasn't even going to allow herself to think about it.

'Could I have a bag for the dress?' she asked, and he pulled an old supermarket carrier bag out of a dispenser inside one of the cupboards and handed it to her.

'I'll see if I can find out about the agents for Mrs Smith's house tomorrow,' he promised. 'I'll give you a ring. Have you got my home number in case you've got a problem over the weekend?'

She shook her head, and he scribbled it down on a sticky note and handed it to her. 'Here.'

Then suddenly there was no more to say, so she

put her shoes on, the heels ridiculously high with the soft old jeans and floppy shirt, and found her car keys in her bag.

'I'll see you on Sunday,' she said, and as she walked to her car, she could feel his eyes on her. She slid behind the wheel and glanced up at him, but the light threw shadows across his face and she couldn't read his expression.

He lifted a hand in farewell, and as she drove off she experienced a sudden, unheralded pang of loss, almost as if she missed him already.

How ridiculous! Of course she didn't miss him! He was a colleague. A workmate. A fellow professional.

Of course she didn't miss him.

CHAPTER THREE

NICK phoned Helen at ten o'clock on Saturday morning, to tell her the name and number of the estate agent, and then for some reason he didn't end the call. Not that he seemed to have anything in particular to say, except that Mr Emanuel was all right and recovering well in hospital, and he told her a little more about the room in the surgery which would be her temporary home. Then he seemed to grind to a halt, and to fill a slightly awkward silence, she said, 'I'll wash your jeans and shirt and bring them back with me on Sunday.'

'Don't bother,' he said, in a curiously gruff voice. 'They look better on you than they ever did on me anyway.'

She felt a gentle tide of warmth wash over her skin at his words. There didn't seem to be anything to say, no sensible way to reply, so she said nothing and the silence dragged on. Finally he cleared his throat.

'Well, if you haven't got any problems, I'd better go and get on with the tree-house. I'll see you tomorrow evening. Why don't you come for supper? We'll eat about seven o'clock.'

'Thanks,' she said, suddenly short of air. 'I'll do that. Good luck with the tree-house.'

He chuckled. 'Thanks,' he said. 'I'll need it.'

Helen hung up, settling the receiver back with a

little click and staring pensively at it. She had a perfect vision of Nick in the garden with Sam, building the tree-house in the fork of an old apple tree, with a wonky rope ladder and a little door just big enough for Sam to get inside. It was just the sort of thing she'd always wanted as a child, the sort of thing she would want for her own child, but she doubted her ability to build it safely.

And she had yet to convince the adoption authorities that she would be a suitable parent anyway. She sighed and ran her hand through her hair, lifting it away from the nape of her neck. It was hot again today, close and sticky, and the thought of her new tangled rose garden was wonderfully enticing.

She phoned the estate agent, and to her delight he thought the cottage would sell at auction for a figure in her price range. If she was successful, she could take possession of it as soon as all formalities had been completed, although, of course, there was a great deal of work to do before it would be truly home.

Still, she would only be at the surgery a few hours a day, and would have plenty of time to spend on it in the afternoons and evenings, so with any luck wouldn't be too long before it was done. She was suddenly excited, and couldn't wait for Monday evening.

A whole new chapter of her life was about to begin, and she didn't allow herself to ponder on how much of her excitement was because Nick was going to be at the centre of it.

Because, of course, he wouldn't be. She had an

agenda already, clearly mapped out and planned, and Nick wasn't part of it.

'Focus,' she told herself firmly, and tried to think of everything she'd have to do before the adoption authorities would consider her.

Saturday was a scorcher. Nick found himself out in the garden with Sam, wedged halfway up a tree, screwing together a platform to make the base of the tree-house while most of his mind was perversely fixed on Helen.

His head was full of images of her—her long legs as she climbed out of her car, her face as they walked through the garden of Mrs Smith's cottage, kneeling beside him on the blood-splattered floor helping him with Mr Emanuel, and then late on Friday night, wearing his shirt and the worn-out old jeans he'd discarded years ago, taut across the smooth curve of her bottom.

Even the thought filled him with heat. On a hot day like today, that really wasn't an asset, and it did nothing for his concentration.

'Dad!' Sam wailed. 'You've cut this one too short, so it doesn't fit.'

Nick groaned. 'Never mind, son, we'll use it somewhere else. We've got plenty of planks to choose from.' He went down the ladder and selected another length of wood, cut it to the right length and screwed it into position. 'Right, I reckon we're about ready to build the sides. How tall does it need to be?'

'I dunno. Big enough for me to sit in, but not too high 'cos it'll look silly. And I want a window looking that way.' Sam pointed across the garden towards the woods.

'What about the door? Which way do you want that to face?'

'Down the drive,' Sam said firmly, 'so I can see you coming.'

Nick nodded. 'OK. Right, let's get to it.'

And if I get really lucky, he thought, I won't hammer my thumb too many times, thinking about Helen.

By Sunday afternoon the tree-house was finished, and Sam was installed, with an old piece of carpet cut to fit, and a collection of odd cups and plates so he could take friends up there for picnics. He was up there now, with Tommy from over the road, and every time Nick stuck his head out of the door he could hear them giggling.

He was glad he'd finally got round to it, after all the nagging, and they really did seem to be having fun.

Unlike Nick.

He was busy cooking supper, wondering why on earth he'd asked Helen to come and join them. It wasn't that he didn't like cooking, because he did, but it was too hot still, and he knew he was going to ridiculous lengths in order to impress her. What he couldn't quite work out was why, but he had a horrible feeling it was connected with his hormones.

Every time he thought about her, his body leapt to attention, awakening sensations and emotions that had been dormant for years, ever since Sue had died.

Not that it wasn't about time, of course. Five years

alone was long enough for anybody, and he was only thirty-six now, far too young for his sex life to have been mothballed all this time. Still, his social skills were rusty, because it had been over ten years since he'd tried to impress a woman, and he wasn't at all sure he could remember how to do it.

And maybe stunning her with his cooking wasn't the way to go—always assuming he could, of course. Knowing his luck, she'd be a vegetarian or have a wheat allergy. Oh, well, you couldn't win them all.

He turned his attention back to the prime fillet of local barley-fed beef, spreading it thickly with pâté and then wrapping it in Parma ham. It needed twenty-five minutes in a hot oven, but he wouldn't put it in until Helen was here. He was serving it with new potatoes roasted in olive oil and herbs and garlic, and a mixed green-leaf salad, in deference to the appalling heat. He'd made a summer pudding the night before, and it was chilling in the fridge, the rich dark red juices soaking into the white bread and butter that lined the deep bowl. He just hoped it would hold together when he turned it out, but he probably wouldn't get that lucky.

Not today, not when it mattered.

Not that it ought to matter. He wondered what he was doing. She was going to be a colleague, and he really, really ought to concentrate on that fact, and not allow himself to become sidetracked by her body—or his!

He glanced at his watch. It was half past five, and he was cooking pizza and chips for the boys. He'd take it up to the tree-house with some lemonade in a minute, and then at half past six Sam was going back to Tommy's house for the night and would go to school with him in the morning. That would give Nick the evening free to settle Helen in, and then sort her out early in the morning.

Not to mention giving them an opportunity to eat together alone. In fact, if he helped her move her things in before they ate, then they would have the rest of the evening together without interruptions.

The phone rang and he picked it up.

'Hello?'

'Nick? It's Helen. I wondered—would it be a real pain if I came a little earlier? I've got everything loaded in the car and I could leave now, if that wouldn't be a problem. It actually only takes about forty-five minutes, once you know the way.'

'That's fine,' Nick said, thinking on his feet. 'I just have to see Sam and Tommy over the road after they've eaten, and then we could go straight to the surgery and settle you in before supper. How would that be?' He found himself holding his breath waiting for her reply, mentally berating himself for allowing it to become so important.

'Oh. Um, yes, OK, that would be fine,' she said, and he let his breath out on a quiet sigh.

'I'll look out for you in three-quarters of an hour, then,' he said, trying not to sound too eager. Difficult, when he was panting like a choirboy in a brothel. Oh, hell. He cradled the phone, whipped the pizza and chips out of the oven, slashed the pizza into bits and piled everything on a tray, grabbed a bottle of lemonade out of the fridge and headed up the garden.

The tree-house ladder was a few strips of wood nailed onto the trunk, and he struggled up it, leaning his chest against the tree and juggling the tray at arm's length. All he needed was to dump all of it on the floor, but he got away with it. Sam and Tommy lunged out of the doorway, grabbed the tray from him and disappeared back inside the tree-house with a whoop of delight. He passed the lemonade to them, sprang down from the tree and headed back to the kitchen.

Ten minutes later it was spotless, the salad was made, the new potatoes were parboiling ready to roast and he just had time to plump the cushions in the sitting room before he heard the scrunch of Helen's tyres on the gravel drive. He drained the potatoes, threw them into the pan of oil, put the saucepan into the dishwasher and had the front door open before she reached it.

Nick's heart thumped against his ribs, and he felt the slow burn of desire warm his body yet again. She looked even more lovely than he'd remembered, and he suddenly had the horrible feeling that he could be in deep, deep water. Hot water. Totally out of his depth. Oh Lord, Sue, help me, he thought. You'd know what to do.

But Sue wasn't there, or he wouldn't be in this mess. The thought sobered him, and he dredged up a smile. 'Hi, there,' he said, and opened the door wider. 'Come on in. You made good time.'

'I was probably speeding a little,' she said with a wry grin. 'Anything to get the air moving through the car. I can't believe it's so hot.'

She didn't look hot, just windswept and absolutely delectable. She handed him a carrier bag.

'Here, your jeans and shirt. I've washed them.'

'I told you not to bother. The jeans don't fit me any more, I've outgrown them,' he said with a wry grin. 'You might as well keep them—the shirt, too. I never wear it any more. Anyway, the colour looks better on you. That muddy olive green just makes me looked dead.'

'Are you sure?' she said. 'I love the shirt.'

'Quite sure. Just have it,' he said, suddenly irritated. He really, really didn't want to think about how good she looked in it, with the soft fabric draped over the ripe curve of her breasts. He'd been tortured by the memory all weekend as it was.

'I'll just go and sort the boys out,' he said, 'and then we can go and move your things into the surgery. I won't be long.'

'Where are they?'

'In the tree-house. They've just had pizza and chips and lemonade, so they'll probably be sick, but it won't be me that has to clear it up.'

Helen laughed, a warm, rich chuckle that made him smile. 'Can I come, too? I'd love to see the tree-house.'

Nick shrugged. 'Yeah, sure. It's nothing amazing, I can assure you.'

'It's just that I always wanted one when I was a child, and I love them.'

There was something wistful about her then that got to him, and he felt his smile soften. 'Me, too. I never had one either. A friend of mine did, and I think, adding all the time together, I probably spent a couple of years of my early childhood in it. That's why I made Sam one, because I never had one myself.'

'Living your life through your child?' Helen said with a wry grin. 'You want to be careful, doing that—a child psychologist would have a field day with you.'

'Tell me about it,' he said with a slightly bitter laugh. 'Everybody's so busy being correct these days they'll forget how to be parents. Come on, let's go and find them or the evening will be gone.'

They went up the garden together, and with every step of the way he was conscious of her presence, aware of her in a way he hadn't been aware of a woman for years. He didn't need this, he thought, but her perfume drifted to him on the evening air, mixed with the scent of honeysuckle and wisteria, and it was irresistible.

The boys saw them coming, and there were shrieks and wails and giggles before he eventually managed to persuade them to come out. Helen gazed longingly at the tree-house, that same wistful smile on her face, and he almost wished he'd made it a little bigger so she could fit in it. Maybe he'd make her one in her rose garden.

'It's gorgeous,' she said softly. 'You've done it really well. He's a lucky boy to have you for a father.'

Nick snorted. 'That's not what he said on Friday night,' he muttered to her. 'If you remember, I was the lowest of the low.'

'Ah, but that was my fault. I'm so sorry about that.'

He shrugged. 'What were you supposed to do about

it? Your car broke down. Nobody can help something like that.'

'But when you're eight, things look a little different. As far as Sam was concerned, you'd broken a promise. Kids are very black and white.'

'Sam's getting quite good at the grey areas,' Nick said ruefully. 'I'm afraid he's had rather a lot of practice.' He peered up the tree. 'Come on, boys, time to go.'

With a bit more cajoling and a certain amount of grumbling, the boys were persuaded to come down, and Nick walked them over the road to Linda, Sam's overnight bag dangling from his fingers. Linda invited him in, but he was conscious of Helen's things that still needed to be unloaded, and the supper that he still had to cook, so he declined.

Nothing to do with the fact that he wanted to spend as much time as possible with Helen this evening.

He crossed the road again, and found her bent over a rose in the front garden, her nose buried in the middle of a huge overblown apricot bloom. She straightened as he approached, and gave a lovely smile.

'It smells heavenly,' she said softly. 'I can't wait to get my cottage. There are some fabulous roses in the garden.'

'I take it you're going for it, then,' he said, and tried to ignore the little flutter of hope in his chest. To have her so close...

'Yes—thank goodness he thinks it'll be in my price range. I would have been gutted if it had been too expensive.'

Her and him both, he thought drily. Lord, this was going to drive him nuts.

'Shall we take your stuff down to the surgery?' he suggested hastily, and she agreed.

They only took the one car, and it didn't take long. She didn't have a great deal, and there was very little to show her in the surgery that wouldn't keep until morning. He helped her make up the bed, and she hung up a few clothes before turning to him with a smile.

'That's it, then. All the rest can wait. I'm starving.'

'Good,' he said with a grin. 'I can't bear picky women who fiddle with their food.'

'Not me, then.' Helen laughed. 'I've never been accused of fiddling with my food.'

Maybe his instincts were right. Perhaps he would be able to impress her with his culinary expertise. It was about the only social skill he had in any degree after all, he thought with disgust.

They drove back to his house, parked her car next to his and went in.

'I just need to put the meat in the oven,' he said. 'It shouldn't take long, everything's virtually ready. Make yourself at home.'

Helen settled herself at the breakfast bar with her elbows propped on the counter and her chin in her hands, and she watched him. It was no hardship. He was easy to watch, his movements fluid and confident. He was truly at home in his kitchen, and it was obvious he knew exactly what he was doing. She envied him that.

He was right, it didn't take him long, and he turned to her with a smile. 'Right, that's that. We've got about twenty-five minutes before we eat. Fancy a drink?'

'That would be nice.'

'How about a glass of wine? I've got a nice Merlot that would go well with this, or you could have tea or coffee, or there's iced water or— I don't know, all sorts. You choose.'

'I have to drive later,' she said regretfully. 'Can I save the wine for the meal?'

'Of course you can. So what will you have now?'

Helen shrugged. 'Water?' she said. 'It just tastes different really cold.'

He grinned. 'I agree. That's why I bought the fridge. I could never remember to fill up a bottle, or to use it, and I resent paying good money for bottled water, so I used to drink rubbish. Sam drinks water now all the time, and that has to be healthier than fizzy drinks.' He filled two tall glasses with the cold water and the outside frosted instantly.

He slid one across to her, and their fingers brushed as she reached for it. It was like touching an electric fence, she thought, as the tingle shot up her arm and dithered around her heart. Distracted, she drew patterns in the mist on the outside of the glass with her fingertip, avoiding his eye. Suddenly the kitchen seemed terribly small—too small.

Maybe Nick thought so as well, because he immediately picked up his glass and headed for the door. 'Come on,' he said, 'let's go into the sitting room.'

She followed him through into a lovely room, not

the circular base of the windmill, as she thought it would be, but a large, rectangular room with a fireplace at one end and heavy beams spanning the ceiling. It was simply furnished in muted, natural tones—creams, soft terracotta, a deep, muted jade green on the walls. The carpet was off-white, more of a rug than a carpet, although it covered most of the wooden floor, and she was sure it would feel wonderful to wriggle her toes in.

'What a lovely room,' she said, looking around her at the pictures on the walls and the interesting little pieces of sculpture on the shelves at the end each side of the fireplace.

'Thanks. I like it. It's my retreat, the place I come when I want to relax. I don't get to be in here very often.' His smile was wry, and she answered him with one of her own.

'Maybe that will get better now I'm here to take some of the pressure off you.'

Nick snorted softly. 'I doubt it. It's not work that's the problem, it's running round after Sam all evening that takes the time. And then, of course, at the weekend, he'll find something like a tree-house for me to do.'

'You love it really,' Helen said softly.

'No—I love him,' Nick corrected her. 'Believe me, Helen, being a single parent is no picnic.'

Her smile faded. 'I know. My mother did it.'

'And I suspect that most of the time you were quite unaware of the pressure she was under.'

Helen thought about that for a moment. Had she been? Maybe. Certainly, she'd never been made to feel that she was a burden—any more, she was sure, than Sam was. She settled into a wonderfully comfortable chair opposite Nick, and gave a tiny nod of acknowledgement.

'You could be right. I never really thought about it before.' The admission stunned her slightly, but Nick didn't press the point. Instead, he moved the conversation on and talked about her duties the following day.

'I wonder if you feel up to taking a surgery in the morning?' he said. 'Lawrence is still away, and the locum, of course, is out of the question with his chickenpox, so it would be a real help if you felt you could.'

'I thought that's what I was here for?' she said with a smile.

'I thought you had to go see the estate agent?'

'I do, at some point, but it doesn't have to be the morning. Just so long as I do it some time tomorrow before the auction.'

Nick nodded. 'In that case, then, we'll split the morning surgery between us, and I'll do the house calls. That should give you plenty of time.'

He glanced at his watch. 'I'll just check the oven,' he said, and unfolded himself from the chair, his long legs carrying him from the room in a couple of strides.

Helen looked around her. On the shelves at the end there was a group of photographs, and she stood up and went over to them. A younger Nick, with a pretty woman by his side, clearly in love. The same woman, with a new baby in her arms, and again with a toddler.

A wedding photograph, in a larger frame, stood at the back of the group. Helen ran a fingertip lightly over the glass, tracing their happy smiling faces. No, not happy—radiant.

So radiant that she felt like a voyeur. She took her hand away, retreating from the evidence of so much love, but it seemed to reach out and follow her.

A great well of sadness and loss rose up inside Helen, and she wondered how Nick could cope without his wife. He had clearly loved her very much. What had happened to her? Had she died? Left him? Surely not the latter. Not with that much love inside them both.

'That's Sue,' Nick said quietly from behind her.

She hoped he'd say more to fill her in, but he didn't. The silence was gentle, though, without raw emotion, and she turned to him. 'Where is she now?'

He sighed. 'She's dead. She died in an accident—she was knocked down by a car. Sam was nearly three.'

'I'm sorry,' Helen murmured. She didn't know what else to say, so she said nothing. If he wanted to talk about it, he would.

He didn't. 'Supper's ready,' he said, a little gruffly. 'Come on through.'

The meal was wonderful. She ate far too much, and although at first she'd been worried that the atmosphere might be a little strained and haunted by Nick's wife, in fact it didn't happen. Instead, the conversation flowed easily between them and suddenly it was nearly eleven o'clock and more than time to go.

She'd had three cups of coffee after their dinner,

and she felt wide awake, but she knew she had to get up and work in the morning and she wasn't going to be able to do that unless she got to bed.

'I must go,' she said reluctantly.

He nodded. He saw her out to her car and opened the door for her, and as she slid behind the wheel she looked up at him and smiled.

'Thank you for a wonderful evening.'

'My pleasure,' he murmured. For a moment he paused, and for one crazy instant she wondered if he was going to kiss her goodnight, but then he straightened up, gave her a slightly crooked grin and raised his hand in farewell. 'See you in the morning.'

She nodded, and started the engine, pulling away and turning down the hill towards the surgery. She drove slowly through the quiet little village. Almost all the houses were in darkness, and as she turned into the surgery she was relieved when the outside light came on automatically.

She let herself in through the side door, using the pass key and the code that Nick had given her, and within ten minutes she was ready for bed. She'd do the rest of her unpacking in the morning, she thought, but just for now she wanted to lie quietly and think about her evening with Nick.

But her mind betrayed her, and all she could think about was Nick and Sam, and how they'd lost Sue so suddenly and tragically.

Better to have loved and lost than never to have loved at all? She wasn't sure, but one thing she was sure of. There was a hole in Nick's life, a great yawning void, and she wasn't the woman to fill it.

CHAPTER FOUR

MONDAY morning came all too soon, and there wasn't any time for Helen to dwell on her relationship with Nick. Not that she really had a relationship with Nick, except her professional one, and that was in full swing by nine o'clock.

He'd arrived at eight, before the reception staff, and had found her in the kitchen, clearing up after her breakfast.

'You must have heard the kettle boil,' she said with a smile. 'Tea or coffee?'

'Coffee would be wonderful. How did you sleep?'

'Fine, thanks.'

He propped himself up against the edge of the worktop, his feet crossed at the ankle, accentuating the length of his legs and the leanness of his hips. She looked away, refusing to indulge herself in the luxury of admiring him.

'So,' she said in a carefully neutral voice, 'which consulting room am I going to have for my surgery?'

'The locum's been using the one next to mine, so I suggest you have that,' he replied. 'Lawrence has the one on the other side of the corridor. Feel free to move the furniture round if you want.'

'I'm sure I'll manage.' She handed him the mug of coffee, and he wrapped his fingers round it, held it to his nose and sighed deeply.

'That smells wonderful.' He shot her a rueful grin. 'I confess I overslept this morning. Must have been all that Merlot.'

'Very likely,' she said, returning his smile. 'It's a good job I was driving, or I might have been in the same boat, and you would have come in and found me still in bed.'

He raised an eyebrow just slightly and chuckled. 'That might have been interesting. Maybe next time.'

Helen tried very hard not to imagine the scene, but her inventive mind was working in overdrive and didn't want to co-operate. However, she was rescued from any further potentially embarrassing speculation by the arrival of the receptionist.

The woman bustled into the room, stopped dead in her tracks and stared blankly at Helen.

'Julia!' Nick said with a welcoming grin. 'Just the woman. I'd like you to meet Dr Helen Moore, who's coming to join us in the practice—correction, has come to join us in the practice.' He gave a crooked smile. 'I've managed to twist her arm and persuaded her to start work this morning. She's sleeping in our on-call room until she's made further arrangements for her accommodation.'

Julia's eyes swung from Nick back to Helen. 'Oh! Right. Well, welcome to the practice, Helen. Let's hope you don't regret it. Just make sure Nick doesn't work you to death.'

'On a part-time contract? I think I'll probably survive.' She smiled at Julia and held out her hand. 'It's nice to meet you.'

Julia shook her hand and returned the smile. 'Has

he shown you round? The usual trick is to throw new people in at the deep end and expect them to cope, but if you've got any questions, just come and ask me.'

'Thanks. I'll remember that. You might regret making the offer by the end of the morning, though.'

Julia chuckled. 'I doubt it. Anything that takes the pressure off Nick is bound to improve our working conditions. He gets like a bear with a sore head.'

'If you two are just going to talk about me, I think I'll go and get on with my work. God knows, I've got enough to do.'

He straightened up, winked at Helen and left the room, leaving Helen and Julia alone to talk about the practice routine, and giving Julia a chance to fill Helen in with all the things she would need to know.

'Right,' Julia said after a while, 'if that's everything, I need to go and get the phone, and you probably need to look through the notes for your morning surgery.'

Thus dismissed, Helen made her way into the room that was to be hers, sat down in front of the desk and blew out her breath in a long gust. Well, she'd done it. Found a part-time job, started work—well, almost started—and hopefully found a house. Not bad for three days' work. A few minutes later, right on the dot of eight-thirty, she pressed the bell to call her first patient through.

Well, that wasn't too bad, she thought. Of course, until this morning the patients had had no idea that there was a new doctor, and so everybody who'd come in was genuinely ill. Helen knew that once word got around, people would come just to see the new doctor, but until then hopefully she would get only genuine cases, as she had this morning.

Like Mrs Maitland, who'd been concerned about a breast lump, and Mr Jones who'd come back for a check on his BP following a change of medication.

She'd been able to reassure both of them, but it had been less easy to reassure the last patient, an elegant, articulate woman in her sixties. There hadn't seemed to be anything wrong with her, but according to her notes she was a continual visitor, and she seemed to be convinced that she was dying. Nothing Helen had said had made any difference, and the woman had clearly been angling for a referral to a hospital consultant. The trouble was, the only consultant she could justify referring her to was a psychiatrist, and she didn't think that that was exactly what Mrs Emery was after.

She spoke to Nick about it afterwards in the office, and he sighed and ran his hand through his hair.

'Ah, yes, Mrs Emery. I wondered what you'd make of her. What was it this time? Chest pain? Abdominal pain?'

'Headache, actually. I didn't really know what to do, so I ran a few neurological tests and sent her home. She's got to come back next week if it's no better. I told her to take paracetamol once a day.'

'I think the poor woman's problem, really, is that she's just terribly lonely,' Nick said. 'In the good old days, she would have had her family all around her to reassure her that there was nothing wrong, and probably a grandmother or two to look after to occupy her time. As it is, she's got nothing to do, she's a comparatively young widow with plenty of money, and she's basically bored stiff. Maybe we ought to tell her to get a job.'

'Perhaps you could offer her one,' Julia said. 'She could give me a hand. Heaven knows, we're busy enough.'

'What, and expose her to all those potential ailments? Not a chance,' Nick said with a laugh. 'As you're so busy, I don't suppose you've had time to make the coffee, have you?'

Julia rolled her eyes. 'Of course. I never neglect the important things. I was going to bring it through, but you've rattled through your patients so quickly this morning I didn't have time.'

'Wonderful, isn't it? I could get used to this. Any word from Lawrence yet?'

Julia shook her head. 'No, not since Friday. I expect he'll ring later on. You'd better have your coffee quickly, Nick,' she added, 'because you've got quite a few calls to make, and you've got a great stack of admin left over from last week.'

'When haven't I?' Nick said with a groan.

He headed for the kitchen, and Julia and Helen shared a smile. 'He never did like the admin,' Julia said with a chuckle. 'Lawrence usually deals with it but, of course, while he's away it falls to Nick.'

'Poor Nick. I hate admin, too, so I can sympathise. One of the joys, I suppose, of a part-time job. I don't expect I'll have to do very much.'

Julia laughed. 'Don't you believe it. I expect they'll

foist it off on you just as fast as they can.' She cocked her head on one side. 'Nick tells me you're hoping to buy Mrs Smith's cottage.'

'I am. And that reminds me, thank you, I have to phone the estate agent and make an appointment to go in and see him this afternoon. I gather they'd had a survey done.'

'Have they? Probably a good idea. Goodness only knows when any work was last done on it. She was in a bad way, poor old duck. It was a blessing, really, when she died. Of course, if it hadn't been for Nick she would have died there all on her own, but he got her into hospital so she died at least clean and comfortable with her family around her. He was wonderful to her.'

Helen could imagine that. Even from their brief acquaintance, she could tell that Nick had a kind streak about a mile wide, which was probably why Mrs Emery kept coming back to see him. Most doctors would have told her to take a hike, except for the fear of litigation, but she knew that Nick would listen to her, and so she kept on coming back. Maybe he was right, maybe she did just need a job. When she came back next week, which she surely would, Helen would have a little chat to her about her lifestyle and see how amenable she was to suggestion.

In the meantime, she needed to phone the estate agent and sort out her accommodation, or she'd be living in the on-call room for the rest of her contract!

The cottage looked scruffier than she remembered. Of course, she didn't have Nick with her to distract her, or point out the good features. That probably made a difference, and also the fact that in her hand she had a copy of the survey which showed an inordinate amount of work to be done. Nothing very expensive, but a relentless list of things she'd have to tackle one after the other. Some of the window frames, a part of the roof, repointing on a small back wall, as well as all the plumbing and electrics which she'd expected.

Still, she loved it, and the garden was, if anything, even more beautiful. She wandered down to the end and looked over the fence, and she realised that she could see the window in the tree-house. Sam would be able to watch her while she worked on the garden, and she'd be able to wave to him—and, coincidentally, keep an eye on him. Not that she thought Nick didn't keep an eye on him properly, but where the tree-house was situated, it was just out of Nick's range of vision.

This all assumed, of course, that she actually managed to outbid everyone else for the house. The survey felt heavy in her hand, not only because of the weight of the paper but also the weight of the contents. Taking on a project of this magnitude on your own was somehow far more daunting than sharing it with a partner, but she didn't have the luxury of a partner and she wasn't going to. She went back into the kitchen and looked around it.

The one good point was that it had an Aga. There were lots of bad points—the units, the sink, the dripping tap, the uneven floor—the list was almost endless. Nevertheless, it looked out over the garden, it was big enough to have a table in it, and there was a huge range of kitchen units available very reasonably from any number of shops.

Nothing was impossible, she reminded herself. She could do it. Even on her own, she could do it.

And maybe if she told herself that enough times, she'd believe it.

With a heavy sigh Helen left the house, locked the door behind her and drove back to the estate agent to return the key. Then, without any further prevarication, she signed the necessary documentation that would enable her to bid at the auction.

As she turned into the surgery car park Nick was just leaving, and he paused and smiled at her.

'All set for the auction?' he asked.

'Well, I don't know about set. I'm scared to death, actually. I've just been round there again, and it looked much worse today.'

'It'll be fine,' he said comfortingly. 'If there's anything you can't manage, I'll give you a hand, if you like.'

'Really?' She stared at him in amazement. 'Why would you want to do that?'

'Why not?' he said with a shrug. 'After all...' he smiled '...we'll be neighbours.'

'You must be crazy,' she said. 'I've been hearing about how good you were to Mrs Smith. You really, really don't want to start waiting hand and foot on her successor.'

He tapped her on the end of her nose with a blunt forefinger. 'Let me be the judge of that. What are you doing now?'

Helen shrugged. 'I don't know. I thought I'd have

a cup of tea, and then maybe after the auction drive around and get to know the village a little, perhaps have supper in the pub? I haven't really planned it.'

'You could join me for supper,' Nick said. 'It won't be anything special, but you're more than welcome. You can tell me all about the auction.'

'What about Sam? Won't he mind me coming round again?'

'He has homework on Monday night. Reading or something like that. He'll be fine. It was only on Friday that he wanted my undivided attention. He's got his wretched tree-house now, so maybe I'll get a bit of peace for a few days. Who knows?' He grinned. 'Anyway, it's up to you. I eat at about seven during the week, but if you're going to come I'll wait.'

'I don't suppose you could keep me company at the auction, could you?' she asked, feeling another flutter of nerves.

He shrugged. 'Maybe. I'll ring my parents and see if they can hang onto Sam, and I'll call you here if there's a problem. The auction's only in the village pub, so we could walk.'

He slid behind the wheel of his car, raised a hand in farewell and drove out of the car park, leaving her in suspense. Part of her wanted him to come, but the other part, the part with self-discipline, thought she ought to go to the pub on her own and keep out of their lives.

She knew what she ought to do. Still, having Nick with her would be a great support, and maybe there'd be time for him to run through the survey before the sale. Then if there was anything in there that she'd overlooked, maybe Nick would be able to help find it before it was too late.

At ten to six, chastising herself for her weakness, Helen turned onto Nick's drive and parked her car. The front door was open, and she called out as she entered.

'In here,' Nick called, and she followed his voice to the kitchen. He was fiddling with salad things, chopping and slicing, and he looked totally at home.

'Were your parents OK to have Sam?' she asked, but he shook his head and her heart plummeted. She couldn't do the auction alone!

'No, but Linda was, so he's round there with her and Tommy. It's better, actually. He loves it there, it's his second home. He'll be back later. Have a pew.'

'This is getting to be a habit,' she said with an apologetic smile. 'You do realise I've eaten with you every evening since I came for interview, except for Saturday when I wasn't here?'

'It's my magnetic personality,' he said with a crooked grin. 'Must be. It can't be the cooking, we're having fish fingers and oven chips tonight. Still, I've made a salad as my concession to vitamin C.'

Helen smiled and hitched herself up onto a bar stool, propping her elbows on the breakfast bar and feeling very much at home. 'I'm sure it'll be lovely, whatever it is.'

'You're too kind. Water?'

Was she really so predictable? Probably. 'Thanks,

that would be lovely,' she said with a smile. She looked around his kitchen, and he pulled a face.

'Don't look too hard, it could do with a jolly good scrub.'

'I'm looking for ideas,' she said. 'Not that a new kitchen is very high on my list of priorities at the moment. I've got rather more immediate worries, like the roof.'

'I thought she'd had the roof done?'

'Only part of it, apparently. The little back bit still needs doing, and it needs some repointing round there as well. Then there's all the wiring, and the plumbing—'

'I think I'd better read this survey,' Nick said with a grimace. 'It sounds a bit of a horror. No wonder you were put off.'

'I wasn't exactly put off,' she protested. 'Just—'

'Put off?' His smile was teasing, and did funny things to her knees. It was a good job she was sitting down. She rummaged in her handbag and pulled out the survey, pushing it towards him across the counter.

'Read it for yourself. It's enough to give you nightmares.'

He flicked through it, alternately frowning and raising his eyebrows, and then he put it down. 'It's not that bad,' he said. 'I think the guy's just a pedant. I'm sure if you go round the house and look at the things he's picked up, you'll find that most of them aren't that bad.'

'I wish I had your faith.'

'Perhaps it's just experience. I've done loads of DIY in my time. When Sue and I bought this place, it was virtually derelict, and we did a lot of the early work ourselves together. Then when she died it gave me something to do, so I spent the next two or three years finishing it off. You'll find two things about DIY. Most things are easier than you think, and all of them take longer. Oh, and did I mention that the Law of Sod applies?'

Helen laughed. 'Tell me about it. I've done a little bit of DIY myself, but nothing like this. I just hope I'm not biting off more than I can chew.'

'Well, if it helps, I really meant what I said about helping you, and I've got lots of useful things like drills, sanders, and so on. You're more than welcome to borrow anything you need.'

He glanced at his watch, then met her eyes with a grin. 'Right. Let's go and buy you a house.'

Helen's heart was in her mouth. She picked up her number from the auctioneer, took her place in the seething throng of bidders and curious onlookers, and waited for her cottage to come up.

The bidding on a pair of cottages was brisk, and an ex-pub went for something a little over the guide price. She felt her shoulders droop. What if she didn't get it?

'Right, ladies and gentlemen, Rosemary Cottage, Post Mill Lane, for the executors of Mrs Hilda Smith. Where will you start me?'

He threw numbers at the assembled company, dropping his price until someone picked up the gauntlet. There was a nod to Helen's right, then one straight in front of her. It was still well below the guide price, and she bided her time, her heart hammering.

'Any advance?' the auctioneer asked, his hammer poised, and Nick nudged her.

'Yes!' she called, her voice a little frantic. She waved her number at him, and he nodded. The other bidder looked at her, then back to the auctioneer and nodded again.

She nodded ferociously, and the other man must have realised she had the bit between her teeth, because he shook his head and turned away.

'He's a property developer,' Nick muttered. 'He can't afford to be sentimental.'

Neither could Helen, but suddenly that was nothing to do with it, because she was in this to the death. She would outbid them all—

'Going twice...' There was a crash, and Nick turned to her with a grin.

'Congratulations. You're the proud owner of Rosemary Cottage.'

She looked at him in blank astonishment. 'Really? What about the others?'

He shrugged. 'No others. I think they took one look at you and gave up.' He grinned and prodded her towards the auctioneer's assistant. 'Go and do your stuff. I'll buy you a drink.'

On trembling legs she made her way to the auctioneer's desk. They were selling a Georgian vicarage now, the reason, she guessed, why most of the people were there, and the bidding was fast and furious. She fought her way through the crowd, still convinced that there had been a mistake, but the lady behind the desk smiled at her.

'Ah, Dr Moore. Congratulations. Could you sign here?'

And that was it. The cottage was hers—or would be, as soon as the banks opened and the money could be transferred. With a huge sigh of relief, she made her way back to Nick, just as the hammer came down on the vicarage and the place went into uproar.

They swallowed their drinks and walked back to Nick's house, Helen unnaturally quiet beside him.

'Penny for them?' he murmured, and she shot him a rueful grin.

'Just wondering if the bidding was so slow because the others saw something in the survey that I missed.'

He shook his head. 'No. It's just that it's small— and anyway, they were all there for the vicarage. There's been a lot of hype about it for the past few weeks.'

'I hope you're right.'

'Of course I'm right. We'll go over to the cottage after supper and have a look, set your mind at rest.'

'Or not,' she said philosophically.

He unlocked the door and they went into the kitchen. The oven was hot, and he slid the tray of oven chips and fish fingers into it, fiddled with the salad and handed Helen the cutlery.

When it was done he dished up and took his place at the breakfast bar beside Helen.

It seemed oddly familiar. He was getting altogether too used to having her sitting there next to him. As she'd pointed out, she'd been there three nights out of four, and it was in danger of becoming a habit.

Still, he reminded himself, there was a good reason for it tonight, and as soon as their simple meal was cleared away, he intended to go back to the cottage with her, survey in hand, and try and allay her fears.

Just as they finished the doorbell rang, and he went and opened the door to find Linda there with Sam and Tommy.

'Dad,' Sam said hopefully, 'can Tommy and I go and play in the tree-house now? I've done my reading.'

'Are you quite sure?' Nick eyed his son with scepticism. 'You haven't been watching telly?'

Sam wriggled uncomfortably. 'That was after I finished, Dad,' he protested. 'I have done it, really.'

He met Linda's laughing eyes over their heads. 'He has done it, I promise,' she assured him.

'OK, then. Thanks for looking after him. I'll walk Tommy back in a bit.' He looked down at Sam. 'I tell you what, read me a page, then you and Tommy can go and play.'

A disgruntled Sam rummaged in his bag, emerging a moment later with the book in hand. Nick threw Helen an apologetic smile, but thought it wouldn't do her any harm at all to see the real side of parenting. It was one thing playing with tree-houses, it was quite another attending to the nitty-gritty of your child's education.

It didn't seem to worry her, though, because while they were sitting at the breakfast bar, reading, she cleared away the plates, loaded the dishwasher and put the kettle on.

There was something terribly homely about it, and she'd slipped into their routine absolutely seamlessly. It ought to worry him, but it didn't. On the contrary, it seemed utterly right, and rather distracting.

So distracting that he actually didn't notice how far down the page Sam had read, because he simply wasn't concentrating on the child. He forced himself to pay attention to the last few lines, and then with a smile of relief he let the boys go.

They shot off, and Nick grinned at Helen. 'That's that out of the way. Thanks for clearing the dishes.'

She smiled back. 'My pleasure. If you're going to keep feeding me, it's the least I can do.'

He stifled the retort that he'd be happy to feed her for ever. He had a feeling she wouldn't want to hear it. 'Let's go and have a look at the cottage,' he said instead. 'It's close enough to the tree-house that they'll be safe.'

Five minutes later, they were walking through the gap in the fence and through the tangled garden, key in hand.

'Are you sure the owners don't mind you taking me in?' Helen asked. 'After all, I haven't paid yet. It seems a bit cheeky.'

Nick shook his head. 'I spoke to the son today, in fact, and he's quite happy. I think, after all this time, they trust me, and anyway they're delighted that you wanted to buy the house. I told him you were a keen gardener, and he seemed very pleased. He grew up here, and he remembers his mother planting a lot of the roses. He said he hoped you'd get it.'

He let them in through the back door, walked through the house with her room by room and, one by one, he despatched each of the surveyor's comments. Then they went outside, and he did the same thing again. 'Look on the bright side,' he said confidently. 'There aren't any structural faults.'

Helen raised an expressive eyebrow at him. 'No, of course not, that would just be the icing on the cake.' She rolled her eyes. 'It's quite bad enough as it is,' she wailed. 'How much worse could it possibly get?'

Nick opened his mouth to answer but she laughed and clapped a hand over it.

'No! Don't tell me!' She laughed. 'I don't want to know!'

His hand came up and circled her wrist, gently easing her fingers away from his mouth. Suddenly, the atmosphere changed and, instead of easy camaraderie, the air became charged with tension. Her eyes met his, wide and slightly startled, and her lips parted a fraction.

It was too much for him. With a quiet groan he drew her into his arms and lowered his mouth to hers.

She tasted wonderful. Her lips were soft and warm, parting further to allow him access, and she slid her slender arms around his waist and drew him closer. The slow simmering burn he had struggled to control for the last four days raged out of control, threatening to consume him. The feel of her ripe, firm body pressed against him nearly drove him wild, and all the suppressed needs of the last five years rose up to torment him.

'Helen,' he groaned against her lips, and a little whimper rose in her throat. It nearly killed him.

He wanted her in a way he'd forgotten he could want, and only the thought of the boys in the tree-house just a short distance away prevented him from laying her down in the long, damp grass and making love to her there and then. Reluctantly, he lifted his head and stared down into her wide, confused eyes. She gazed at him for a startled moment then looked away, lowering her eyes and taking a slight step back, putting distance between them.

He supposed he ought to apologise, but he was damned if he was going to. She kissed like an angel, and there was no way he could talk himself into re-gretting it.

'Um—I should be getting back,' she said hurriedly. She sounded a little puzzled, as if she wasn't quite sure what had happened or where it had come from.

He caught her hand as she stepped away from him and halted her flight. 'Helen, don't.'

She looked back at him, her eyes now wary. 'Nick, I have— We— I don't do this sort of thing.'

'What sort of thing? I kissed you.'

She gave a strangled laugh. 'I did notice.'

He smiled a little crookedly. 'Good. I would have hated you to miss it.'

She shook her head slightly as if to clear it. 'Nick, really, I didn't mean to— We shouldn't have.'

'Helen, it was just a kiss.'

A kiss he was at pains to repeat at the earliest opportunity, but he had a horrible feeling he wasn't going to get a chance. Oh, hell. He stabbed a hand through his hair, and went to pick up the survey which lay forgotten on the grass.

'Well, if you've seen enough of the cottage, I suppose I should get back to the boys.'

'Yes, thank you.' She was suddenly formal, all the familiarity of suppertime gone, wiped out at a stroke.

He felt suddenly very, very sad.

CHAPTER FIVE

HELEN couldn't get the kiss out of her mind. For the rest of that week, she avoided Nick except in a professional context, and even then, all contact between them was limited to what was strictly necessary. The rest of the time, she avoided him, but of course there were times when she couldn't, and then she would find him watching her, a slight reproach in his eyes.

Still, she couldn't explain, didn't want to go into all the reasons why she didn't do this sort of thing. Any sort of thing, really, with men. Not since Tony.

Even his name brought back the sense of betrayal that made her heart pound and her stomach sick with dread and disgust. He was just her father, all over again, both of them lying, faithless bastards, cruel and self-interested.

So she threw herself into her work, and when she wasn't working, she busied herself with planning the work she was to do on the cottage, getting quotes from local contractors and generally throwing herself headlong into the preparation. It served two purposes. The first was to bring forward the date when she could move into the cottage, and the second, and much more pressing, was to keep her out of Nick's way.

By Friday afternoon, the legal work on her purchase was completed, and she spent the weekend stripping wallpaper in the larger of the two bedrooms. By a miracle the electrician was able to start work on Monday, and with any luck she should have the room decorated so she could move into it by the end of the week. Of course, the central heating still needed to be installed, but the plumber couldn't start for another week, and she couldn't stand the tiny room at the practice any longer. It was just too near to Nick.

On Monday, Mrs Emery came back to see her about her headaches. After asking her how they were, Helen sat back in her chair and smiled. 'You do seem to suffer from an awful lot of little, trying ailments,' she said gently. 'It's almost as if you feel slightly under the weather all the time. Is that right?'

'Oh, yes,' Mrs Emery said. 'I just never feel well. Every morning I wake up and I feel—I don't know, just not right.'

'And is that just since you lost your husband?'

Mrs Emery's eyes fell, and she stared at her hands, her fingers twisting together. 'There's just nothing to wake up for any longer,' she said sadly. 'Nothing to do, nobody who needs me, my life's just empty—and on top of that, I feel ill.'

'Maybe you aren't really ill,' Helen suggested, 'but just lonely and bored. I think that's quite understandable. Have you ever thought of getting out of the house and finding something else to do?'

Mrs Emery snorted. 'What, like working in a charity shop? It would drive me mad.'

'How about a proper job? A real one with responsibility—people relying on you.'

'I don't know that I could do it any more. All that

responsibility, I don't know if I could cope with it. But you're right, of course, I'd be much happier if I had something to do with my days.'

'Think about it. See what's around. You never know, it could open up a whole new world to you.' Helen smiled encouragingly at her. 'You see, I really don't think there's anything wrong with you. I'm sure you do get headaches, and tummyaches and perhaps even a little bit of chest pain from time to time, but they're nothing to worry about, and I think if you were busier you wouldn't even notice them.'

Mrs Emery nodded. Helen noticed that her eyes were misted with tears as she stood up to leave. 'Thank you, Dr Moore. I'm sorry to have troubled you.'

'You haven't troubled me,' Helen corrected gently. 'See how it goes. We're always here if you need us.'

She watched her go, hoping that she'd said the right thing. It seemed to have struck a chord, anyway, and it would have given her something to think about.

Helen gave her next patient something to think about as well. He was a child, a boy of about Sam's age, and he came in with a rash on the inside of his lips, on his hands and the soles of his feet. He'd had a headache and a slight sore throat for the last few days, and his temperature had been slightly elevated at the start of the illness.

Helen examined him and turned to his mother with a smile of reassurance. 'He's all right. I think he has a thing called hand, foot and mouth disease—'

'Foot and mouth disease!' the boy exclaimed. 'Wicked!'

'Oh, good grief! How on earth has he caught that?' his startled mother asked.

Helen stifled a smile. 'No, not foot and mouth disease, it's hand, foot and mouth disease. It's quite different; it's caused by the Coxsackie virus, and it's pretty harmless usually. The incubation period is three to six days, so if any of you are going to get it, you'll probably do so quite soon. Just keep him off school until it's cleared up, and make sure he washes his hands very thoroughly when he's been to the loo, and don't let him cough all over people.'

'Can you give him anything for it?'

Helen shook her head. 'No, it isn't necessary anyway. He should be fine in a day or two. Give him paracetamol if he's uncomfortable or if his temperature rises, but otherwise it's just a case of waiting it out.' She turned to the boy with a smile. 'You'll be fine in a couple of days.'

'Wait till we tell Dad I've got foot and mouth disease!' he said with a grin, and Helen shook her head.

'Don't forget the hand,' she reminded them. 'You don't want to panic people, and you'll have the press after you if you go round saying that.'

'Cool,' he said. 'I'll be famous!'

'Notorious, more like,' his mother said with a sigh.

'You can get a rash on your buttocks with it, too,' Helen pointed out. 'Perhaps we should rename it hand and bottom disease, to distinguish it!'

They left, still chuckling, and Helen stacked the notes together and sat back with a sigh.

He had been her last patient of the morning, so she shut down her computer, gathered up the notes and her coffee-cup and went out into the office. Julia greeted her with a grin.

'I gather young Tim's got foot and mouth.'

'Hand, foot and mouth,' Helen said with a sigh. 'I wish I'd just told her it was a virus now. It'll be in the papers next and I'll get the sack.'

'I doubt it. Oh, by the way, Nick wants to see you. He's in the kitchen.'

Helen gave a mental shrug. It was probably something about work—maybe Mrs Emery. She went into the kitchen, and found Nick busy making coffee. He glanced at her over his shoulder and smiled cautiously.

'Hi there. Coffee?'

'Thanks. I gather you wanted to see me?'

'I did. You saw Mrs Emery. How was it?'

She shrugged, relieved that that was all he wanted. 'I don't know. I asked her if all her symptoms started after her husband died, and she started talking about how empty her life was. I suggested that maybe filling it with a job or some other activity might help her, just by keeping her so busy she didn't notice all the little things that were wrong with her, and she went away to think about it. I made sure she knew she could come back, though, and I'll probably live to regret it.'

Nick chuckled softly. 'No doubt. You might be lucky, though. We might all be lucky if it works.'

'I felt sorry for her.'

'Tell me about it. I know exactly where she's coming from,' Nick said in a quiet voice. 'Still, she'll get there in the end. It just takes time.'

He passed her a mug of coffee, and as she took it their fingers touched and she all but snatched it from him. The contact was too much, reminding her yet again of the kiss, of all the things she couldn't have. She avoided his eyes, and with a slight sigh he sat down at the table and set his mug down with exaggerated care in front of him.

'How's the cottage coming on?' he asked in a neutral voice.

She picked up his cue, latching onto the innocuous subject with gratitude. 'I don't know. The electrician starts today—or, hopefully, started. I'll go up there in a few minutes and have a look.'

'Of course, it's yours now, isn't it? I must give you back the key.'

'There's no hurry, any time will do. Bring it into work when you remember.'

A slightly awkward silence settled over them, and she couldn't think of a single thing to say. Her coffee was too hot to drink quickly, and so she was trapped with him, stuck there until she was able to make her escape.

Nick stirred his coffee pensively, then lifted his head and met her eyes, his mouth tilting into a slightly crooked smile.

'I'm sorry,' he said softly. 'I shouldn't have kissed you. I didn't mean to do this to us. It was just—'

'Forget it,' she said, cutting him off. 'It doesn't matter.'

'Oh, but it does,' he murmured. 'It matters, because all I can think about is that I want to do it again.'

Helen felt heat stain her cheeks. She remembered

the kiss, remembered the feel of his mouth on hers, the sensation of his body against her own, the touch of his hands in her hair. She wanted him to do it again, wanted to feel it all over again, wanted more— far more. Much more than was sane or sensible.

'No.'

He sighed and ran a hand through his rumpled hair. 'I know,' he said softly. 'It's all right, Helen, I'm not going to do anything. You're quite safe.'

Perversely, she was disappointed. She didn't want to be safe. She wanted him to kiss her again. She drained her coffee, burning her throat in the process, and pushed back her chair. 'I'm going to the cottage,' she told him. 'I don't know when I'll be back. Just lock up if you want to go.'

She changed into jeans and a T-shirt, drove the short distance to the cottage and found a white van outside. She parked behind it and went in to a scene of absolute mayhem. Boards were up, wires dangled and there were piles of plaster on the floor near every doorway. She could hear a man whistling upstairs, and she ran up and found the electrician busy threading wires through a hole in the floor. He looked up with a grin.

'Hi, there. All right?'

'Yes, thanks. How're you getting on?' she asked him.

'OK. It's only tiny, isn't it? Shouldn't be long really. Two more days? Oh, and the plumber dropped in. He could start tomorrow, if you like. He's had a cancelled job. He wants you to ring him.'

'Excellent. Thanks, I'll do that.'

That meant she could move in even sooner, she realised with relief.

Helen went back downstairs and out into the garden, looking around her with enthusiasm. The first thing it needed was a jolly good weed, the grass mown and some of the shrubs cut back, but she'd have to consult her books to make sure she did any pruning at the right time of year.

She needed garden tools, and her own, like practically everything else, were now in store. Nick would have some that she could borrow, of course, but she didn't really want to ask him. In the meantime, though, she was wasting an opportunity to get in amongst it, so she got back in her car, drove to the nearest garden centre and bought herself a border fork, a little trowel and a bucket to put the weeds in.

Then she went back to the cottage and set about weeding the rose bed. By the time the electrician left at five, she'd freed the first few rose bushes of the choking undergrowth, and she sat back on her heels and looked at her handiwork with a feeling of satisfaction.

She was hot, sweaty and ready for a shower, but she was making real progress at last. She got stiffly to her feet, wincing as the circulation was restored and her legs were attacked with pins and needles. She carried the full bucket of weeds down to the spot she'd chosen at the end of the garden for her compost heap and tipped them out, stunned at the size of the heap she had already created. By the time she finished the whole garden, the compost heap would be taking over the world. Still, it had to be done.

In a foolish and sentimental mood, she picked a few of the roses and stuck them in the milk bottle on the kitchen window-sill. No doubt the electrician would laugh at her tomorrow, but it couldn't be helped. It was her home, and she couldn't wait to be in it.

Suddenly, she heard childish voices on the other side of the fence, and she saw Sam and Tommy peeping out of the window of the tree-house. She waved to them, and they waved back, and she smiled. Then she heard Nick's voice, and her smile slipped a little. His face appeared over the fence, his eyes wary as if he wasn't sure of his welcome.

'How are you getting on?' he asked.

'OK. The electrician's been working all day, and I've started weeding. The grass could do with a good cut, but I don't have a mower at the moment so it'll have to wait.'

'I'll run over it for you, if you like,' he offered.

Helen hesitated, unwilling to use him, and he gave a crooked smile.

'Stop thinking, Helen. Just say, "Yes, please, that would be lovely."'

'Yes, please, that would be lovely,' she said with a wry smile. 'Thank you, Nick.'

'Any time. I told you that.'

He vanished, and a few minutes later she heard the rattle of a mower being wheeled along the gravel path. Then the fence panel disappeared and he pushed the mower in. 'Got a compost heap?' he asked, and she pointed to the growing pile in the corner.

'Excellent.' He started up the mower, and began

running it up and down the grass, making neat stripes in the lush green sward. Half an hour later, she had a lawn instead of a meadow, and she'd weeded a few more of the roses. The garden was starting to look like a garden, and she probably looked like a tramp.

'There you go, all done.' He gave her his cock-eyed grin, and as usual it went straight to her knees. She propped herself up on the fork.

'Thank you, Nick. It looks much better.'

She thought he'd go then, but he didn't, he stayed, wandering round the garden and looking at the tangled mass of shrubs and perennials that flopped across the path. She wanted him to go, but she didn't know how to ask him without being rude, and so she carried on with her weeding, ignoring him and hoping he'd go away.

He appeared at her side, crouching down beside her, his face almost at her level.

'You look as if you could do with a shower and a good meal,' he said softly. 'Why don't you go and get cleaned up while I cook you something?'

She was horribly tempted, but she really ought to resist. 'I thought we'd discussed this?' she said a little desperately.

'No, we discussed the kiss. We didn't say anything about a neighbour cooking you a meal when you'd been working hard.'

'Nick…' She looked up at him, all ready to argue, but that lazy crooked smile and the kindness in his eyes undid her.

'Thank you,' she said wryly, quietly resigned. 'I'm

starving, and I'm sick of take-aways and pub meals. Supper would be lovely.'

She must be crazy. All the time it had taken her to shower and change, she'd been telling herself she was mad. Now, as she waited outside Nick's door, she knew it. Her heart was pounding, her breath was jamming in her throat, and she couldn't understand for the life of her why she'd agreed to it.

He opened the door, looking cool and relaxed in freshly pressed trousers and a checked shirt, open at the neck. He'd changed, and she was glad now that she'd made a little more effort when she'd dressed. Not that it mattered, she told herself sternly, but she couldn't help noticing his appreciative eyes as they tracked over her.

The outfit was simple, just a pair of cream cotton trousers with his loose, floppy, olive green shirt over the top, but it seemed to please him.

'I'm wearing the shirt,' she said unnecessarily, and he smiled.

'I noticed. It looks good on you.' He stepped backwards into the hall and gestured towards the kitchen. 'Come on in. I'm still tinkering about with the salad. Sam's gone to Tommy's.'

So they would be alone again. Her heart thudded against her ribs, and she drew a steadying breath before following him into the kitchen. Once there, she sniffed appreciatively.

'Smells good,' she said with a strained smile.

'That's just the marinade,' he told her. 'I've made up some kebabs to put on the barbecue, and I've got spicy chicken wings and some wicked sausages from the butcher in the village.'

'Good grief,' she said weakly.

'Well, you said you were hungry,' he said with a smile. 'Can't have you fading away.'

She found herself perching automatically in her usual position at the breakfast bar, watching as he opened the bag of mixed lettuce leaves and shook them out into a big bowl.

'It's a lazy way of doing it,' he said with a grin, 'but I don't care. I can't be bothered to buy five different kinds of lettuce.'

'Don't apologise to me.' She smiled. 'I always buy it like that. Is there anything I can do? I always end up sitting here, watching you.'

He shook his head. 'Don't worry about it, there's very little to do. It's just nice to have company.'

It was. She'd had a week of lonely evenings, and it made a pleasant change to have someone to talk to. Odd, her evenings had never been lonely before. It was strange how suddenly being alone had become being lonely, just since she'd known him.

Disturbing, really. Worrying.

'Right. I think we're ready to put some things on the barbecue. Could you bring this tray for me?'

Helen picked up the tray and followed him out into the garden, round the corner to the patio. The barbecue was gas-fired, and he'd already lit it, so it was ready to go. Soon the air was full of that wonderful, summery smell, and she sat in a comfortable wooden armchair and sipped a glass of wine while he turned the kebabs and prodded the sausages and generally did man things to the food.

She suppressed a smile. It was funny how a barbecue brought out the cook in men, she thought, although she already knew that Nick liked cooking. She wondered if he always had, or if it had just been necessity that had taught him. Whatever, she wasn't going to complain, because the food smelled fantastic and she was absolutely ravenous.

After a few minutes he handed her a plate piled high with barbecued goodies. 'Come on, then, help yourself to salad,' he ordered, and she tucked in, only too willing.

'Gorgeous,' she said around a mouthful of food.

He chuckled. 'I take it that was a compliment,' he said with a grin. 'I didn't quite catch it.'

'Sorry,' she said laughingly. 'I said gorgeous.'

'I take it you were talking about me?' His eyes were laughing, and he was teasing her, but nevertheless her pulse raced again.

'Your kebabs, actually,' she said lightly. 'Can't see anything else gorgeous around here.'

One eyebrow quirked, but he said nothing, just chuckled again and returned his attention to his food, leaving her in peace to get her scattered emotions in order.

He'd brought fresh strawberries for dessert, from the pick-your-own field just outside the village, and he'd drenched them in thick double cream, with a little sprinkle of demerara sugar, 'just for crunch,' he said with a smile. They were wonderful, juicy and succulent and bursting with flavour, and she ate far too many. Finally, she pushed the bowl away with a laughing groan.

'Enough!' she said. 'I'll burst if I eat any more.'

'Don't do that,' he said calmly. 'I'm not on duty and I don't really want have to clear up the mess.'

'It'll be all your own fault,' she said lazily, sprawling back in the chair and sighing contentedly. 'I could manage a coffee, though,' she added with a grin.

'So demanding,' he murmured, getting up and heading towards the kitchen, but she could see the smile playing round the corners of his mouth and, anyway, she knew she'd only pre-empted him by a matter of moments.

She stacked up the plates and followed him inside.

'In or out?' he asked, and she realised that he'd already made the coffee in the machine, and it was ready to pour.

'In, I think,' she said. 'It's getting a bit chilly outside now.'

Nick laid a tray with the coffee, found a box of chocolate mints and carried them all through into the sitting room. She kicked off her shoes, and curled up in the chair she had sat in before, with her feet tucked under her bottom. He handed her a coffee, offered her a mint and retreated to the opposite chair with his own coffee.

A companionable silence settled over them, free of tension for the first time in a week, and Helen felt herself relaxing. The combination of hard work in the garden and good food and wine was soporific, and after a while she could feel her eyelids drooping.

'Am I keeping you up?' he asked with a smile in his voice.

Her mouth curved lazily. 'Not so as you'd notice,' she said with a chuckle. 'I ought to go home, really. It's just not very appealing, compared with this.'

'I know what you mean,' he said. 'That room serves its purpose, but it was never really designed to be lived in for any length of time. Still, you'll be in your cottage soon, won't you?'

'I hope so. I'm really looking forward to it, but I won't have a kitchen to speak of for a while.'

'At least, if it stays warm, you can cook on a barbecue.'

'If,' she said drily. 'Knowing my luck, it'll pour with rain until December now.'

His mouth twitched into a wry smile. 'No doubt. I've got Sam breaking up for the summer in about a month, and I expect the weather will be foul and he'll be thoroughly objectionable.'

'It's bound to be foul when I have the roof off,' she said. 'That's just the way it goes.'

'Just give me fair warning,' he said. 'I'll make sure he's with his grandparents that week.'

They exchanged smiles of understanding, and he threw her another mint. She nibbled it, making it last, but finally it was finished and it was time to go.

'Nick, thank you for a lovely evening,' she said softly. 'And thank you for cutting my grass.'

'My pleasure—all of it.'

He got to his feet and helped her up, going with her to the door. Her bag and keys were on the table near the door, where she'd put them when she'd come in, and she collected them up and turned to him to say goodnight. He was closer than she'd realised, though, and as she turned she bumped into him and he reached out to steady her.

It was enough. Just that one single touch undermined all their resolve, and the tension was back in spades.

With a stifled groan, Nick lowered his head to hers and their lips met and melded.

He tasted of chocolate and mint and coffee, rich and dark and a little sinful, and the combination was irresistible. He eased her closer, so that her soft breasts were pillowed against his chest and she could feel the pounding of his heart through the soft fabric of her shirt. His mouth nipped and sucked, shifting slightly, leaving her mouth to follow the line of her jaw, down over the soft skin of her throat to the hollow at the base where her pulse beat hard under the skin.

Helen felt the hot, wet trace of his tongue, then a shiver of cold as he blew against the damp skin, and a little cry rose in her throat. He groaned, claiming her mouth again, and his tongue plundered the secret, inner depths. She heard a whimper, probably hers, but she was past caring. They were both adults, Sam was out for the night, there was nothing to stop them.

Nothing except common sense.

What was she doing? She'd promised herself she wouldn't do this, and now she was allowing herself to be sidetracked by the first half-decent man that came along.

With a huge effort of will she pushed him away.

'No,' she whispered.

She could feel his heart pounding under her hands, the ribs vibrating under the onslaught.

'Nick, I'm sorry,' she said unsteadily. 'I really didn't mean to—'

'Hush, Helen, it's all right.' He wrapped her in his arms, folding her against his chest and holding her until their hearts slowed and the screaming need had settled to a steady roar. Then he let her go, brushed a feather-soft kiss over her lips and opened the door.

'Goodnight, Helen,' he said softly.

She didn't speak. She couldn't. Instead, she lifted her hand and touched it lightly against his cheek, then turned away.

Nick watched her go, the ache inside threatening to burn him up. He wanted her, and he knew she wanted him, but for some reason she was holding him at arm's length.

He realised he still knew hardly anything about her—why, for instance, did she want to adopt a child? He didn't know, but instinct told him that until he did he would get no further with her.

And there was Sam to consider.

He realised that his hormones were engaged but his brain was still free-wheeling in outer space as far as Helen was concerned, and it wasn't fair. It wasn't fair on Helen, it wasn't fair on Sam and it probably wasn't fair on him.

Frustration ripped through him, and he went back into the sitting room, turned the music up loud and poured himself another coffee.

He could see the dent made by her neatly rounded bottom in the chair opposite, and he groaned and closed his eyes.

No. He couldn't do this. He had to find out more about her, get to know her.

Back to basics, old man, he reminded himself. Woo her, don't rush her.

Romance her.

He gave a hollow laugh.

If he could even remember how...

CHAPTER SIX

HE WAS different.

For no good reason that Helen could think of, Nick's behaviour towards her had changed.

She noticed it for the first time on Tuesday morning, after she'd stopped their kiss in its tracks the previous night. He wasn't distant, exactly—if anything, he was even more attentive, but it was a different sort of attentiveness. Instead of the teasing, light flirtation of before, he seemed to weigh up what she said, thinking about her replies. It was almost, she thought in surprise, as if he had changed tack and was trying to get to know her better.

How very strange—not that he should bother, but that it should feel so different. She almost missed the flirting, although she tried to convince herself that she didn't, and anyway, this was a side of him that she found very interesting.

They talked about all sorts of things in the little intervals between patients and visits and admin, and on Thursday morning she found herself telling him about her childhood, about how difficult it had been at times and how strange it had been without her father.

'He didn't seem to understand the concept of faithfulness,' she said quietly. 'My mother just took it, over and over again, until finally the last time she threw him out for good. It got even worse then, because I used to listen to her crying at night and I thought I'd been naughty.'

'How old were you?' he asked.

'About eight. Sam's age.'

Nick winced. 'You poor little sod,' he said softly. 'It must have been hell. At least when Sue died we were all able to grieve for her, and there was no anger and resentment and bitterness to deal with.'

'You must have missed her dreadfully,' she murmured.

His eyes clouded. 'I did. I didn't know what to do with myself at first, but you get through it somehow. My parents were wonderful. They moved down here so they could help me with Sam, and they were just amazing. I don't think I would have got through it without them.'

She thought of the photos, of the love shining from their eyes, and she shook her head. 'I don't think I can even begin to imagine what it must have been like.'

'Numbing, really, at first. I didn't feel a thing. Not for ages. It was about six months before I started to feel anything again, and then I just fell apart. We'd had so much, and to lose it all so quickly was awful.' He gave a crooked grin. 'Still, I got there in the end, and I think Sam survived reasonably intact.'

'He seems remarkably well adjusted,' Helen said quietly. 'You must be proud of him.'

Nick pursed his lips slightly and nodded. 'Yes, I am. I'm very proud of him, even though he can wind me round his little finger, and I like to think Sue would be happy with what we've achieved. It's difficult to juggle it, though, when you're a single parent.'

Helen nodded slowly. 'Yes, I can see that it must be.'

'Do you mind if I ask you something?' Nick asked after a little pause. 'Will you tell me why you want to adopt a child?'

She hesitated, then shrugged slightly. She didn't have to tell him everything. 'Because I'm alone. I don't have a partner, and I don't want one, and the thought of going to a sperm bank and having a total stranger's body fluids injected into me in a clinic just makes my blood run cold. Besides, there are so many children out there that need someone, and I've got a lot of love to give.'

Nick was silent for a moment. He was chasing a grain of sugar around on the table top with a blunt fingertip, and after a moment he looked up and met her eyes.

'What if you meet somebody you want to share your life with?'

'I won't,' she said flatly.

'But if you did? Would you change your mind? Would the child be in the way? A child is for life, not just for Christmas, and all that,' he said with a slight smile, but his eyes were serious.

'I thought that was dogs,' she cut in, trying to lighten the mood, but he just shrugged.

'It is—but you can't send kids back to the RSPCA when you get bored or overwhelmed. It's a huge commitment, and I'm not suggesting for a moment that you aren't up to it, but it's a hell of a lot to take on on your own. I love Sam, but even so he can be very trying at times. Starting from scratch with a child you don't know, a child that isn't part of you—that takes a very special kind of person.'

Nick sat back and laughed softly. 'Heavens, this is all getting a bit heavy for a coffee-break. Sorry. I need to get on and do my calls. I'll see you later.' He stood up, squeezing her shoulder gently in passing, and went out, leaving Helen alone with her thoughts.

Nick was on his way out through Reception when Julia caught him.

'Nick, we've had a call from one of your patients, Mr Graham. The home help found him lying on the floor and called an ambulance, but she had to leave before it came, and the ambulance crew can't persuade him to go to hospital. He's in a state of collapse, but he just flatly refuses to go. Would you go? You might be able to talk him into it.'

'Sure. Give me the address, I'll pop in on the way to my first call.'

Julia handed him the notes, and he put them on top of the others and set off. The elderly man was a patient he didn't see very often, but he did know him, and his state of health was pretty frail.

When he went into the house, he found the man sitting in a chair in the living room, a blanket wrapped round him, and the two ambulance officers trying to reason with him and coax him to drink a cup of tea.

'Ah, Dr Lancaster, thank goodness you're here,'

the ambulance driver said with relief. 'We just can't talk any sense into him.'

'Where did you find him?'

'On the kitchen floor. He's hypothermic, he's got a nasty rattle in his chest and he's been drifting in and out a bit. He seems a little confused from time to time, but most of the time he's pretty with it, and we can't force him to come with us.'

'No, of course not,' Nick agreed. 'Hello, Mr Graham,' he said, crouching down beside the elderly man. He took his hand, ice cold, and chafed it gently between his. 'Can you tell me what happened?'

Mr Graham looked at him with rheumy eyes and blinked. 'Hello, Doctor,' he said after a moment.

'What happened, Mr Graham?'

'I don't know. I think I was making a cup of tea.'

'When was this? This morning? Last night?'

'In the night, I think. I don't really remember. I can just remember lying on the floor for a long time, then Jenny came, but she had to go. She only comes just to get me up, so she only has half an hour with me in the morning. I don't know why she called these blokes in.' He waved a dismissive hand at the ambulance officers, and they shrugged and grinned at Nick.

'Well, I think, as they're here, we might as well take advantage of it, don't you?' Nick said persuasively.

'But I don't need to go to hospital,' Mr Graham protested. 'I'll be all right after a cup of tea. I'm just chilled.'

Nick took a deep breath and counted to ten. 'Let

me just have a look at you. I'd like to listen to your chest.' He got out his stethoscope, sounded Mr Graham's chest and then listened to it while he breathed in and out. At least, he would have done if Mr Graham had been able to breathe in and out without going into a massive coughing fit. He sat back on his heels and waited it out, and when the old man was finished, he just looked at him.

'How long have you been like this?' he asked patiently.

Mr Graham mopped at his eyes with a tired handkerchief. 'I don't know,' he wheezed. 'A day or so?'

'How about a week?' Nick suggested wryly. He folded up his stethoscope and tucked it back in his pocket. 'I'm sorry, Mr Graham, but you're going to have to go to hospital. You've got pneumonia, my old friend, and you aren't going to get better staying at home, lying on the kitchen floor all night. Now, can I find you a few things to take with you?'

'I'm not going anywhere,' Mr Graham said stubbornly.

'Well, as I see it, you've got a choice,' Nick said flatly. 'You can go to hospital, or you can stay here and die on your own. Now, which is it going to be?'

'That's a fine way to talk to an old man,' he grumbled, but after a little more fluff and bluster he gave in and agreed to go to hospital. Nick stayed until he was loaded into the ambulance and the doors were shut firmly behind him, just in case he changed his mind again, but finally he was off and Nick was able to continue with his rounds.

On the way to his next call, his mind drifted automatically back to Helen, and their last conversation.

She'd been very emphatic about not having a man in her life—too emphatic. He wondered if it was anything to do with her father's behaviour, or if she herself had had a bad experience. Maybe both, the one reinforcing the other.

How to ask her, though, without seeming to pry—which, of course, was what he wanted to do. Well, not pry exactly, but certainly find out more about why she was so set against the sort of warm, loving relationship he'd had with his late wife. It seemed a tragedy that such a lovely and generous person with so much to give should shut herself away from that amazing happiness.

Because that was what she was intending to do, and taking on a child, although very laudable, was no substitute for the sort of relationship she was going to be missing.

'Fancy a drink later?'

Helen had been in her room when the knock came on the door, looking through quotes from the roofing contractors, and she looked at Nick in surprise. 'Where, at your place?'

'No, I was thinking of a pub. Sam's out tonight and I thought, if the idea appealed, we could take a run over to a favourite watering hole of mine. They do quite good bar meals, and it's got a lovely view from the garden.'

It sounded very tempting, but Helen wasn't quite

sure of his motive. At least, though, in a public place, they were unlikely to get led astray into another kiss.

'I ought to work on the garden really, and I must make sure that the workmen are all right.'

'The workmen go home at five, Helen, and you'll have been working on the garden all afternoon, if I know you.' He gave her a wry smile. 'You don't have to make excuses to me. If you don't want to come, just say so.'

Put like that, it made her feel churlish. She flashed him an apologetic smile. He was only asking her for a drink and a bar snack! 'It sounds lovely, actually. Thank you.'

'Why don't I pick you up from the surgery at half past six?' he suggested. 'I should finish early today, and that will give us both time for a shower before we go out.'

'I'll certainly need one, in this heat, if I'm going to wage war on the weeds again.'

He grinned and winked, then left her, going back into his surgery for his afternoon clinic. She'd just had her lunch and was on her way up to the cottage, and for the rest of the afternoon, in between answering the plumber's questions and fighting with the couch grass in the flower-beds, she pondered on the motive for Nick's invitation.

After all, she'd made it perfectly plain this morning that she didn't intend to get involved in a relationship. Maybe he was going to try and talk her out of adopting a child again but, if so, he was doomed to failure, because she knew what she was doing and her mind was made up.

'Right, I'm off, then.'

She looked up, snatched from her reverie by the electrician's voice. She scrambled to her feet and tugged off the rubber gloves. 'Fine. How have you got on?'

'Almost finished—about another half-day to go. Is the plasterer coming tomorrow?'

'Yes, in the morning. Will he be in your way?'

The electrician shook his head. 'Shouldn't think so. We're used to working round each other, us trades. Occupational hazard,' he added with a grin.

Helen smiled back. 'OK, then, I'll see you after lunch. I have to do calls after surgery tomorrow morning, so I won't be here quite so early. If you've got any problems, can you ring the surgery?'

He nodded, and wandered off round the side of the cottage, whistling cheerfully.

Helen went into the house and looked around. The upstairs seemed completed, everything back in order, and only the downstairs was still in confusion. He'd agreed to come back and do the kitchen when it was refitted, because there was no point in putting sockets where they weren't needed, and once the plasterer had been it would all look heaps better.

She glanced at her watch, and realised with surprise that it was almost six. The electrician had obviously worked late to finish off, and Nick was picking her up in half an hour. She had to lock up the cottage, clear away her tools in the garden, drive back to the surgery and shower and change. She looked regretfully at the almost finished flower-bed. 'Sorry, lupins,' she said apologetically, and fled.

Nick tapped on her door at the surgery half an hour later, just a minute before half past six, when she was just putting the finishing touches to her make-up. 'Come in,' she called, dropping the lipstick back onto the top of the chest of drawers. She gave a last cursory glance at herself in the mirror, then turned to him with a smile.

'All set?' he said, his eyes running over her appreciatively.

Forgetting her resolve to keep her distance, some imp of femininity in her opened her mouth and said, 'Will I do?'

He smiled knowingly. 'Oh, yes, you'll do,' he said softly, and she felt the warmth of his appreciation all over her.

The pub they went to was about half an hour's drive away, set on the banks of a river, and he'd booked a table on the terrace in the shade of a veranda.

The view was wonderful. Stretched out before them Helen could see the broad, flat water of the estuary with the evening sun glinting across it, the chequer pattern of fields on the other side rolling away into the distance. There were boats on the water, from little dinghies to small sloops, all pointing upstream and swinging on their moorings in the ebb tide.

'What a fabulous spot,' Helen said with a contented sigh, and he smiled.

'It is, isn't it? It never used to be like this, but it was taken over a couple of years ago and it's improved enormously. Not the view, of course, that hasn't changed, but they've landscaped the terrace to take advantage of it and the food's much better.'

She scanned the menu and sighed. Spoilt for choice, she thought, and eventually settled on a sea-food salad. It was a wise choice, and tasted wonderful, but, in fact, it could have been anything because all her attention was on Nick.

He was wonderful company, easy and relaxed, and he managed to avoid any controversial subjects for the entire meal. They finished off with coffee and strawberries and cream, and then they strolled along the river-bank, following the sandy footpath up-stream.

There was a little church a few hundred yards away, almost on the river-bank, and it seemed a very strange and lonely setting, a long way from the near-est community.

Maybe it had always served the people whose live-lihoods were on the river—the fishermen, the ferry-men and the local farmers. Whatever, she thought it must be a beautiful spot for worship. The path widened, and Nick fell into step beside her. She lost her footing slightly on the uneven path and reached out to him, and after that their fingers remained compan-ionably linked.

They reached a little bluff where the path rose a few feet above the river-bank, and they sat on it with their legs dangling over the side and looked out over the water.

'It's so peaceful here,' Nick said quietly. 'I love it. I come here every now and again to recharge my batteries and get away from it all for a little while.'

She looked at him, catching a yearning expression in his eyes, and realised that he was lonely. 'You miss her, don't you?' she said softly, and he nodded.

'I miss having someone to share everything with. That was one of the worst things about it, losing the person I bounced ideas off and shared silly little moments with. I used to go home after work and tell her all the crazy things that had happened. Going home to an empty house with Sam—that was the hardest part.'

He fell silent, but then after a moment he started to speak again. 'It seems such a long time ago now. I suppose we're used to it, but there'll always be something missing.' He gave Helen a thoughtful look. 'Tell me about you,' he said gently. 'Why are you so sure there won't be anybody for you?'

Helen gave a soft huff of laughter. 'Because I don't believe in happy ever after,' she said, not hearing the wistful note in her voice.

'You should,' he said with conviction. 'Believe me, it can happen. Sue and I were just two ordinary people, but we had a fantastic marriage. Mind you, we worked at it. It wasn't always that good. I found it difficult at first, but in the end Sue taught me to show my feelings and open up more, and after that we went from strength to strength. We hardly needed to talk, we just seemed to be able to anticipate what the other one wanted.'

'You were very lucky,' Helen said, conscious of a little pang of envy. 'Believe me, that's very rare. Anyway, men like you are as rare as hens' teeth. The vast majority lie and cheat and sleep around.'

Nick gave her a searching look, and she wondered if she'd sounded as bitter to him as she did to herself. 'I take it you're speaking from experience?' he murmured.

She gave a quiet snort. 'You could say that. My father, for instance—he was hardly a good role model, and since then...' She fell silent, but Nick wasn't going to leave it alone.

'Tell me,' he prompted softly.

Helen shrugged. 'There's nothing much to tell. It's the same old story. I fell for a man, he lied to me and I only found out when I met his wife.'

'I'm sorry.' His arm came round her and he gave her shoulders a gentle squeeze.

'It's OK. It was a long time ago now, but I'm not in a hurry to repeat the experience.'

'Well, if it's any help, you know I'm not married,' he said with a fleeting smile.

No, he wasn't, he was just in love with his dead wife, and there was no way she could compete with that. She got to her feet.

'Can we go?' she said, suddenly in a hurry to get away.

He stood up, brushing the dust off his seat, and gave her crooked grin. 'Running away?' he murmured, but she ignored him and turned away, walking quickly back towards the pub. He followed her slowly, rejoining her beside the car a few minutes later.

Helen was standing gazing out over the water, her arms wrapped around her waist, hanging onto her control. He was getting under her skin, weakening her resolve, and she was suddenly scared that she was going to fall for him and be hurt all over again.

She heard the dull clunk of the central locking, and got into the car, fastening her seat belt with a defiant click.

He drove her back in silence, but instead of returning her to the surgery, he drove to his house.

'Where are we going?' she demanded as they passed the surgery entrance.

'I would have thought it was obvious,' he said mildly.

'But I want to go back to the surgery,' she protested, panic rising in her.

'No, we need to finish this conversation,' he told her with quiet resolve, 'and we can do it here in comfort and privacy.'

Finishing the conversation was absolutely the last thing she needed, but there was no point in arguing with him. He'd made up his mind, and she sensed there would be no changing it until he'd had his say.

With a resigned sigh she got out of the car and followed him into the house.

She was running scared, Nick thought. She looked wary, avoiding his eye, holding herself a little aloof. A bit of him felt guilty for hijacking her, but somehow he couldn't help himself. It seemed so sad for her to be so alone and so unhappy—because she *was* unhappy, he could tell. He knew all about it. He'd had plenty of experience and practice.

He went into the kitchen and put on the coffee-machine. 'Fancy a glass of wine or brandy?' he asked her, but she shook her head.

'No, thanks. I'm all right.'

Helen was far from all right, but that was a completely separate issue. He poured himself a small brandy, found the chocolate mints and ushered her through into the sitting room. She went to her usual chair, kicking off her shoes and curling her feet up under her bottom. She looked at him defiantly, and he gave an inward sigh.

'Don't look at me like that,' he said with gentle reproach. 'I only want to talk to you.' He sat on the sofa and patted the cushion beside him. 'Come here,' he ordered softly.

For a moment she didn't move, but then she unravelled those wonderful legs and crossed the room, curling up at the other end of the sofa, out of reach. She was like the wary, shy little cat his mother had owned once, desperate for affection but hardly daring to come close enough to allow it. He would just have to be patient, but it wasn't in his nature.

He sipped his brandy and rested his head back against the sofa. 'So, how's it going?' he asked. 'The job, I mean.'

She stared at him in surprise, her eyes puzzled, then she gave a little shrug. 'OK, I think. I'm enjoying only doing part time, especially at the moment with the cottage to sort out.'

'How are they all getting on in there? Is it plastered yet?'

'No, the plasterer comes tomorrow. Hopefully it'll start to look a bit better then.'

'You're doing wonders in the garden,' he told her. 'I looked over the fence when I got home from work tonight, and I could see from the size of the compost heap how hard you've been working. Don't wear yourself out.'

'Don't worry—I won't. Anyway, you're only worried because you don't want to have to do my job as well as yours.'

Nick chuckled. 'Too right. It took long enough to find you, I'm not going to let you knock yourself up now.'

He rolled his head back against the sofa again, closed his eyes and sighed. 'I must say, it's a great relief to have you on the team. Did I tell you, by the way, that Lawrence is back on Monday?'

'Julia told me. You must be glad. You can hand back all the admin.'

'What a blissful thought. I can hardly wait.' He took another sip of brandy, and put his glass down, turning half towards Helen. 'So, this bastard who screwed your life up,' he said evenly. 'Tell me about him.' He watched her withdraw, pulling herself in tighter, and then she dragged in a shaky breath and looked down into her glass.

'I met him through a work colleague. He was charming, quite ordinary but somehow different. He made me feel special.'

The words were said with a trace of bitterness, and Nick wanted to kill the man. He bit the inside of his cheek to hold back a vicious retort and concentrated on his brandy, giving her time.

'We had an affair. He said he loved me. We were

going to get married once his mother died. She was elderly, frail, very clingy. He couldn't upset her.'

'So you never went to his house.'

She looked up at him, as if she was surprised he was there. 'No. I never went to his house. Of course not. Then I went to a party held by a friend. Not really a friend,' she explained, 'just someone on the fringes of my circle. I still don't know why, unless it was because she knew and thought it was time I did. Anyway, I got chatting to a woman there, a pleasant woman who talked about her husband and children as if they were the centre of her world, and then Tony came into the room and she turned to him with a smile and introduced him to me.

'"This is my husband," she said, and she was so proud of him, but all I could think was, He's my Tony, the man who loves me but can't take me home because he lives with his sick and elderly mother. Tony, the man who would marry me when his mother died, which she would do soon, but he couldn't shock her by telling her about me—*my* Tony, only he wasn't mine, because he was Jan's, and Jan loved him, and he probably didn't even have a mother.'

Helen floundered to a halt, and Nick reached out and put a warm, comforting hand on her bare foot, hitched up on the cushion beside him. It was icy cold, and she looked shocked. Poor girl, he thought. Poor, poor girl. What a bastard.

He hoped Tony didn't have a mother, because no mother deserved to see her beloved son turn into such a rat.

'So what did you do?' he asked.

'Do?' She looked at him, glazed. 'Nothing. I smiled politely, and made excuses to leave the party, and I drove home. I don't quite know how. Then he rang me, came round, pleaded and crawled and grovelled, but it didn't work. It wouldn't. I knew by then that he was just like my father, and all I could think about was Jan and the children—especially the children. I never saw him again.'

Nick rubbed her foot gently, soothingly, and after a moment she glanced up and gave him a crooked smile. 'So there you have it. The story of my life. Well, my gullible folly, anyway.' She drained her glass, the brandy making her eyes water slightly.

'The coffee will be done by now,' he said, his voice a little gruff. 'Are you sure you don't want one?'

'I will, actually,' she relented. 'Just a small one.'

'Stay there,' he ordered. 'I'll fetch it.'

It was ready, the tray was laid, but Nick stayed out there for a moment, his head resting back against the wall, struggling with a mixture of anger and overwhelming pity.

How could he do that to her? Lie to her like that, cheat her of her emotional security? Cheat him, because he knew now that he would have a hell of a battle on his hands to defeat that much pain and hurt. He'd known pain, but not the pain of betrayal. Sue had always loved him unreservedly, and he'd trusted her, and her him. Helen would probably never trust again.

He shrugged away from the wall and picked up the tray, his mouth a grim line. Lighten up, he told himself. Enough nitty-gritty.

When he came back from the kitchen Helen was nibbling on one of the chocolate mints, and he put the tray down on the floor by the sofa and took one of the mints from the cushion in between them and put it in his mouth, crunching it twice before swallowing it.

'You're supposed to savour them,' she told him, but he just gave her a crooked smile.

'They aren't even a mouthful,' he pointed out, willingly allowing her to sidetrack him.

'You're just not a connoisseur, are you?' she said with a chuckle. 'You're meant to suck them. You can dunk them in your coffee as well. They're nice like that, too.'

'Disgusting,' he said, pulling a face, but he wasn't really serious. 'Chocolate biscuits, yes, but mints? They just melt and fall in the coffee.'

'Ah, but only if you leave them in there for too long. With practice, you can get it just right.'

He couldn't hide the smile. It was such a silly conversation, and as it went on he could tell she was relaxing. Not much. Not really. The slightest word out of place, and he knew that her wariness would be back in spades. He picked up a mint, dipped it in his coffee and held it out to her.

'Open wide,' he said, and she opened her mouth and he put it in, his fingers brushing her lips as he did so.

Heat flared in her eyes, and her breath seemed to catch. His certainly did. The need raced through him again like an express train, and with a short sigh he put his coffee down, moved the box of chocolates and removed her mug from her hand.

'Come here,' he said gruffly, and drew her into his arms.

She came without argument, her body turning so that she lay across his lap, her head resting on the arm of the sofa, looking up at him. Her shirt was gaping slightly between her breasts, and he could see a small peep of lace on the edge of her bra. He almost groaned aloud. His hand trembling, he threaded his fingers through her hair and sifted it. It was like silk, falling in a soft curtain from his fingertips, and with an uneven sigh he bent his head and took her mouth with his.

She parted her lips, and Nick took instant advantage, deepening the kiss. She moaned softly and arched against him, and he could feel the soft press of her breasts against his pounding heart. Unable to resist, he slid his hand up under the edge of her blouse and cupped her breast. A shudder ran through her, and he found the catch of her bra and released it. The warm, soft weight of her spilled into his hand, her nipple peaking against his palm, and he lifted the fabric aside and lowered his mouth to suckle her.

She cried out, awash with sensation, and he eased his mouth away, laying a soft trail of kisses over the smooth skin of her midriff. He covered her again, returning to her mouth and kissing it gently, tenderly, bringing her slowly back to earth.

He didn't want to hurry her, do too much too soon, because she would only hate him for it later and he didn't want that. This love-shy, beautiful woman was worth waiting for, and he would wait for as long as it took to win her and teach her to trust again—even if it killed him.

His kisses changed, gentling, becoming tender and soothing instead of white-hot, and gradually Helen's heart slowed and the ache eased.

She lay there in his arms for a while, and then he dropped a kiss on her hair and lifted his head.

'Time for bed, princess,' he said softly. 'I'll take you home.'

She didn't want to go, but she knew it made sense. This was just her hormones talking, and she could deal with them. She'd been ignoring them very successfully for years.

She stood up, realising as she did so that her bra was undone. Colouring softly, she refastened it and straightened her blouse, slipped her shoes on and ran her hands through her hair.

'I must look a wreck,' she muttered, but he shook his head and smiled.

'You look lovely,' he said gruffly, and heat rocketed through her again.

He drove her home, saw her in and kissed her lightly on the lips, then left her. She got ready for bed and slipped between the covers, lying there thinking about their conversation. She hadn't meant to tell him about Tony, not really, but now she had, perhaps he'd be able to understand her better.

Although maybe not. Her words may have warned him off, but her body hadn't. She thought back to their kiss, to her response to his gentle love-making, and felt the heat wash over her once more. Without words, they'd both said plenty.

It wasn't the answer she'd meant to give him, though, not the answer she'd wanted him to have. It was just her body talking. Her heart was too battered to get involved again, to risk another foray into loving. Would Nick understand that from her sorry, sordid little tale?

She hoped so because, despite the enthusiasm of her body, she really meant it. And yet that wasn't the impression she'd given at all, she realised, heat flooding her at the memory of their kisses.

Betrayed by her own emotions, she turned her face into the pillow and groaned. She hadn't meant to do that, hadn't meant to fall for the lure again. It didn't fit in with her plans.

She rolled onto her back and stared at the darkened ceiling. Did it really matter, though? Just because she had no intention of getting married or becoming involved in a serious relationship with a man, it didn't preclude her from enjoying a little light flirtation from time to time, and after all, for heaven's sake, he'd only kissed her!

She rolled onto her side, thumped the pillow and refused to think about it any further. It was just a kiss. Nothing more. Hardly anything at all. After what she'd said, he'd have to be a fool to misread it.

Wouldn't he?

CHAPTER SEVEN

HELEN woke on Friday morning feeling far from re-freshed. Her night had been full of restless images, and the main feature in her picture-show strolled into the surgery at eight o'clock, looking cool and relaxed and altogether too delicious. Nick's eyes searched her face, gentle humour lurking in the depths of them, and his smile was slightly teasing. However, Julia was there, so he said nothing beyond, 'Good morning, Dr Moore.'

'Good morning yourself,' she said a little grumpily.

'Didn't you sleep well?' he asked, the smile play-ing around his mouth.

'I slept very well,' she said with a saccharine smile. 'How about you?'

'Oh, I slept like a log,' he said, and then added in a murmur, 'Except for the dreams.'

She felt herself colour softly, and turned away to hide her smile. She was conscious of Julia in the background answering the phone, definitely within earshot, and she headed for the door hastily.

'Fancy a drink of something before we start?' she threw over her shoulder, as much as anything to get him and his teasing mouth out of Reception before he said anything else, and he nodded and followed her.

'Tea or coffee?' she asked, but he just smiled and drew her into his arms.

116

'I'll settle for a kiss,' he murmured, and claimed her lips.

She pushed him away with a breathless laugh and turned to the kettle. 'Repeat, tea or coffee?'

'Coffee.' She heard the scrape of the chair behind her as he settled himself at the table, and then the rattle of a magazine.

She plonked the coffee down on top of the magazine and sat down opposite him. He peered at her from under his eyebrows. 'Was that a hint?' he asked with a quirk of his lips.

'Whatever gave you that idea?' she asked, struggling to hide her smile. Damn, she didn't want to seem too pleased to see him, even if she was.

'I can't imagine.' He picked up the coffee, folded up the magazine and put it one side. 'So, how are you?' he asked softly.

'Tired,' she said frankly. 'It must have been all the coffee I had last night, keeping me awake.'

Nick's smile indicated that he didn't believe a word of it, but he was kind enough not to say so. 'Are you OK to do the calls after surgery this morning?'

'Sure. I said I would.'

He shrugged. 'I just wondered, with the builders—'

'They know I won't be there till later. They're going to ring the surgery if there are any problems. Hopefully there won't be, there haven't been up to now.'

'Are you hoping to move in this weekend?'

Helen gave a little laugh. 'Well, I had rather hoped to, but it all depends on how much mess the plasterer's made and if I actually have any power or water. Anyway, my stuff's all in store, so I can't arrange to get it here until next week. I don't know. I might just spend the weekend clearing it up, ready for the removal men next week.'

'Well, if you need a hand, give me a shout. I'll have Sam, but I expect Tommy will come and play with him and they'll probably be in the tree-house anyway, and it's easier to keep an eye on him from your end of the garden. I'll do anything from painting to pruning, but don't ask me to pull out weeds. It's the only thing I really hate, but anything else…'

'Thanks,' she said with feeling. She was beginning to get rather daunted by the whole prospect of decorating the entire house from top to bottom—it might only be tiny, but it still seemed to have an awful lot of walls.

And besides, having Nick's help meant having Nick around, and that was suddenly very appealing. The idea of having an affair with him with no strings attached was growing more tempting by the minute. She drained her coffee, put the empty mug into the sink and smiled at him cheerfully.

'Hi-ho, hi-ho,' she sang, and went out of the room, with the sound of his chuckle following her down the corridor.

Helen's surgery that morning was mostly routine, and filled with a plethora of summer ailments. Athlete's foot, insect bites, a bad case of sunburn and a woman who came in smothered in a fine pinprick rash from head to foot, worried to death that she'd caught

German measles, as she was in the early stages of pregnancy.

'I've had a rubella injection, so I shouldn't have it, but it just seems like exactly the same rash.'

'Not exactly,' Helen said, pressing her finger into the rash and lifting it to watch it fade. 'It's much too solid and even for that, and as you've been vaccinated I think it's most unlikely. Anyway, you aren't unwell. Have you been in the sun recently?'

'The sun? Well, yes, I was sunbathing all day yesterday. But it doesn't really feel like sunburn.'

'That's because it isn't,' Helen told her. 'It's solar urticaria. It just means your skin's reacted to the sun, and in future it would be a very good idea to cover yourself in a high protection factor suncream. I think you'll find that if I give you an antihistamine it should settle very quickly. If it doesn't, by any chance, then please come back, but I really don't think you can possibly have rubella.'

Helen handed her patient the prescription and sent her on her way, then gathered up her notes and left her room. She had six calls to make, and she had to ask Julia directions to most of them. She was getting to know her way round the village, but some of the calls were to outlying villages and isolated farms, and she had no idea where they were.

She decided to do the closer calls first, and then head out into the country, as there didn't seem to be any urgent priority. However, by the time she found her last and very carefully hidden farm, it was almost two o'clock.

It was up a long drive, the farmhouse tucked away

inside a little wood, and as she pulled up a pack of scruffy dogs rushed out and jumped up at the car. She eyed them warily. They were barking ferociously, their lips curled up, and they looked as if they meant business. She tooted her horn, and a lanky youth with a shotgun broken over his arm ambled round the corner and strolled up to the car. She wound the window down a crack.

'I'm Dr Moore. I've come to see Mr Palmer,' she yelled over the barking of the dogs.

He shouted at them, kicked one for good measure and it ran away with a yelp. The others sloped off, and she opened her car door with caution. One of the dogs barked again, but they left her alone and she followed the silent youth into the house.

'Up there,' he said tersely, jerking the butt of the gun towards a door in the wall. She opened it to reveal a narrow, twisting staircase that ran up behind the chimney to the floor above. She climbed the stairs, and as she reached the top the stench was unimaginable.

'Mr Palmer?' she called. 'Can I come up, Mr Palmer? It's Dr Moore.'

'In here,' a querulous voice replied. 'Taken your bloody time, haven't you?'

She held onto her temper with difficulty and followed the smell and the voice to the bedroom. 'I'm sorry, I got held up and then I couldn't find you. You don't have a sign by the end of the track.'

'No. Don't want to attract all those agricultural reps. They come here bringing disease, selling all sorts of stupid gadgets and putting ideas into every-body's heads. Damn nuisance, they are.'

She didn't bother to comment. There didn't seem to be anything she could say that he would want to hear. She put her bag on the floor and opened it, getting out her stethoscope. 'Right, Mr Palmer, what can I do for you?'

'You're the doctor, you tell me,' he said awkwardly.

She looked at the notes. 'It says here you've got a bit of chest pain.'

'Well, I reckon I've got a bit of chest pain, then, haven't I?'

Her grip on her temper was getting more tenuous by the second, but she took a deep breath and counted to ten. 'Can you describe the pain to me?'

'It hurts,' he grunted.

'Can you be more specific? Is it in the centre? High up? Low down? Is it like a band round your chest, or a weight on the middle of it?'

'It's better now.'

She arched a single brow, and he looked away from her, unbending enough to add, 'It was in the centre, like a weight.'

'Did it go down your arm?'

He nodded. 'It did, a little bit.'

She took his pulse, listened to his chest and then folded up her stethoscope and put it away. 'Well, Mr Palmer, I think you've probably had a mild heart attack. I'd like you to go into hospital for a check-up, just to make sure everything is all right. They probably won't keep you in for long, but I think it would be a good idea.'

'I don't have time to go to hospital.'

'I don't suppose you've got time to die either, but nobody will ask you about that one.'

'Are you threatening me?' Mr Palmer asked her, and she shook her head.

'Not at all. I'm just giving you the facts. If you have had a heart attack, and you don't rest, you could die. Your heart needs time to recover, and you may need drugs to prevent it happening again. Now, it's up to you. I can't make you go to hospital, I can only advise it.'

'Better go, then, han't I?'

Behind the bluff and bluster, she realised he was just a frightened old man, and she dredged up a smile. 'You'll be all right, Mr Palmer,' she reassured him. 'It's just a precaution. Do you have a telephone I can use to call the ambulance?'

'Downstairs.'

She closed her bag, went down into the filthy kitchen and found the youth slouched over the kitchen table, skinning a rabbit. 'How's Dad?' he grunted.

'I think he's had a slight heart attack, so I'm sending him to hospital just to be on the safe side. Can you show me where the phone is, please?'

He jabbed a bloody finger towards the wall, and she picked up the filthy receiver with her fingertips and keyed in the number of the ambulance control. She gave them all the details, then took her farewell, unwilling to stay there a moment longer.

She was relieved when she got back to the surgery

and could take a shower. She was sure the smell would be in her car for ever, and she was really glad she'd made it her last call. She changed into her jeans, T-shirt and trainers, and set off for the cottage with all the car windows open, very conscious of how late she was.

However, all was well, and the plasterer had almost finished. The plumber was done, all bar the kitchen, so she had a nice shiny new bathroom with hot and cold running water, and all she had to do was tile it. Like the electrician, the plumber would come back when the kitchen was refitted to finish off. In the meantime, he'd made a temporary connection to the old sink, so she had hot and cold water in there as well.

So all she had to do was decorate it, and refit the kitchen, and the inside would be finished.

All!

Never mind. She had all the time in the world, and she'd be able to have it exactly as she wanted. She went out into the garden until the men had finished, and then she locked the cottage and went to the nearest DIY store to look at tiles.

They had white ones on special offer, very simple ones with a slightly rippled surface that would disguise the fact that she couldn't put them on straight. She picked up loads of them and a huge pot of adhesive and grout in one, then on impulse she added a few boxes of border tiles at hideous expense because they were so pretty.

She piled everything in the trolley, added a few

cans of not-quite-white paint and brushes and rollers, and headed for the checkout.

As she was unloading the things from the back of her car, Nick appeared as if by magic and helped her, taking the heavy boxes of tiles two at a time and stacking them in the hall outside the bathroom.

'I gather you had to see old Mr Palmer today?' he said over his shoulder, and she shook her head.

'He'd had a heart attack. What a place. I thought I'd never find it.'

'I wouldn't have sent you there if I'd known. I would have gone for you—they're a funny lot. A bit of incest, a bit of inbreeding. They've been known to shoot at reps that stray onto the farm by accident. The oldest son's in prison for that.'

Helen shuddered. 'Thanks for telling me. The son greeted me with a gun.'

'Loaded, I have no doubt. Did you go upstairs?'

'I did—and it's an experience I'm not in a hurry to repeat!' she said with a laughing grimace.

'Mrs Palmer died in the bedroom.'

'Recently?' Helen asked with only an element of jest. 'The place smelt horrendous. I don't suppose they've changed the sheets in years.'

He chuckled. 'Oh, well, the health visitor or community nurse can go in there and sort them out. Did you admit him?'

'Eventually. I didn't bother to be subtle. I told him he'd die.'

'He'd understand that. I should think it worked a treat.'

'Absolutely. He folded like a wet tissue.'

'Attagirl. Right, where do you want the paint?'

She shrugged. 'I don't know. I thought I might start upstairs, to give the plaster in the sitting room and hall time to dry. What do you think?'

He nodded. 'Sounds good. You can get the bedrooms sorted out and work your way down. After all, you won't have time to use the sitting room much anyway for a while, but you want to sleep here as soon as possible, don't you?'

Her grin was wry. 'Is it so obvious?'

'Well, you have told me,' he pointed out gently, 'and having stayed in that room in the surgery myself in the past, I do understand.' He carried the paint upstairs, piled it in the centre of the smaller bedroom and then dusted off his hands.

'Right. That's that. How about supper?'

She tipped her head on one side and smiled at him quizzically. 'Are you intending to feed me every night?'

His smile widened fractionally. 'You guessed.'

She shook her head slowly in disbelief. 'You're crazy.'

'So—supper?' he repeated, and she laughed and gave in.

'Supper would be lovely. Let me treat you. I can take you out.'

'Uh-uh. I've got the boys,' he reminded her, as if she needed any reminder with them charging around in the little bit of woodland at the end of Nick's garden and hollering like Tarzan out of the tree-house.

'Then let me get a take-away,' she insisted, but again he shook his head.

'I've got a chicken in the oven, and jacket potatoes. I know it's been hot, but somehow chicken doesn't seem as hot as other things and I'm sick of salad. And the boys insisted on a frozen chocolate gateau from the supermarket, so that's taken care of, too, before you suggest it.'

Helen went through the fence with Nick, leaving her car locked up on the drive of her cottage, and while he put the finishing touches to their meal, she took up her position on her perch at the breakfast bar and sipped a glass of wine.

She was getting terribly used to it, rather too much so, but until she had a kitchen of her own it was difficult to reciprocate—and anyway, she had to eat somewhere, and Nick was only too willing to oblige. She was sure it was only his natural kindness that led him to keep issuing invitations—either that, or the prospect of another stolen kiss.

'There must be something I can do to earn my keep,' she said with a smile.

'Well, if you really insist, you can peel a few carrots, but that's the only thing that still needs doing.'

'I'm sure I can manage.' She slid off the stool, stationed herself at the sink and held out her hands. 'Carrots? Peeler?'

'Such a nag,' he grumbled, dropping carrots in the sink and handing her a potato peeler. 'Anything else?'

'A pan to put them in?'

He slid a pan across the worktop towards her, picked up his glass of wine and went and sat at the breakfast bar, watching her.

She didn't mind. It felt good to be doing something useful in the kitchen again, after such a long time without one. She didn't count the little kitchen at the practice, because she hadn't ever prepared a proper meal in it.

'I'm really looking forward to having my own kitchen again,' she told him as she worked.

'Have you decided what units you're going to have?' he asked her.

She shook her head. 'Not really. I want something tough, and I want it to look in keeping with the cottage, so I thought I might go for a paint in the Shaker style. I don't know. There are lots of them about to choose from. Where did you get yours from?'

'This?' Nick looked around the kitchen. 'My father and I made it. He's always done a little cabinetmaking as a hobby, and it gave us both something to do after Sue died. He made it, I just put the screws in.'

Helen was stunned. 'It looks really professional.'

'That's because of the extravagant granite worktop,' he said with a grin. 'It was the only surface I could think of that I wouldn't burn holes in, so I bribed our local monumental mason to make one for me. It made a change from gravestones and, in fact it's now the major part of his business.

'A lot of his work comes from word of mouth, from people that have seen this and other kitchens he's done, but I don't think he thanks me. The slabs of granite are so enormous in a big kitchen that he keeps wrecking his back. I keep telling him he needs another assistant with a bit more muscle, but he says his wife's more obedient than the average assistant and he can manage. He's a good craftsman, though.'

'Maybe I should get him to look at my kitchen,' she suggested. 'Or maybe I'll just see how expensive the roof and the repointing is going to be before I get carried away.'

'You could always mix it up, with a bit of granite where you're going to make pastry and either laminate or solid wood for the rest of the kitchen. That can look quite good and it's much cheaper.'

'I think I'm getting ahead of myself here,' she said with a grin. 'I've hardly got running water! Right, your carrots are done. Shall I put them on to cook?'

'In a few minutes. Come for a walk round the garden with me first.'

It was the first time she'd really walked around his garden. She'd been to the end, and seen the treehouse, and, of course, walked through to her cottage, and she'd sat on the patio and had a barbecue with him, but she'd never really studied the borders, smelled the roses, enjoyed the clever juxtaposition of colour and form that made up the framework of the garden.

'Who designed it?' she asked him, foolishly hoping it wasn't Sue, although his late wife's garden had nothing to do with her feelings for him, surely, especially if they were just going to have a no-strings affair.

'Designed?' he said with a chuckle. 'I don't know about designed. My mother and I threw a few plants in round the edges, and I laid the turf, but apart from that it's just happened over the years, really. I have a girl who comes in and wages war on it once a week, and I cut the grass, but it's very easy to look after. It has to be. I'm not really a gardener, although I do like sitting in it, and there's a lot of it to look after.'

He glanced towards the tree-house. 'Let's go and get the boys. It'll take them five minutes to come in, and they have to wash their hands, and by the time they've done that the food'll be on the table.'

They had supper in the dining-room, with Sam and Tommy still chattering nineteen to the dozen. She met Nick's eyes over their heads and her heart thumped against her ribs. It was so cosy, so homely and domesticated, and anyone looking in through the window would think that they were the epitome of the nuclear family. How wrong they would be.

She didn't allow herself to dwell on the fact that it saddened her. Being a family with Nick was no part of her plans.

By Sunday evening, Helen had painted her bedroom, and Nick had tiled the bathroom for her. It looked wonderful, and she was delighted that she'd chosen the border tiles. They really made all the difference. She was also delighted that Nick had stuck them on, because he'd done a wonderful job, much better than she could have done, and the result was stunning.

'Now I really owe you a meal,' she said with a smile, propping up the bathroom doorway.

He paused in the act of clearing up the little off-cut pieces of tile and threw her a grin.

'I'll hold you to that one of these days.' He straightened and groaned. 'Not tonight, though.

Tonight, all I can cope with is a hot bath, a nice brandy and some undemanding television.'

'A bath sounds wonderful, but I haven't got any towels here, and I don't have a curtain, and since I don't intend to give the neighbours a peep show I guess I'll just have to go back to the surgery and shower.'

'Spoilsport,' he said with a smile. 'Maybe the neighbours would like a peep show.'

'Pervert.' She grinned.

'No, just hopeful.'

He threw the last broken pieces of tile into an empty bucket and picked it up, swept bits of dust into a dustpan, tipped it into the bucket and moved towards the door. She was standing in the way, and as she leaned aside he squeezed past her, brushing against her. Tired as she was, her body reacted to him, and she felt her heart skitter in her chest.

'You could always come back to my place for a bath,' he suggested, pausing beside her on the landing. 'I expect you could do with a long soak, too, and we've got two baths, so it's not a problem.'

She was incredibly tempted, and it didn't take him long to persuade her. Once again leaving her car on her drive, she followed him down the garden in the dusk, slipping through the gap in the fence and making their way to his house. An owl hooted as they walked, and on her own, she realised, she might have felt a little nervous. As it was, with Nick at her side, it just felt romantic.

'It was good of Linda to have Sam again so you

could help me,' she said as they went in. 'I ought to get her a little something as a thank you.'

'That would be nice, but I doubt if she expects it. We often help each other out.'

'Yes, but this time she helped me, and I owe her.'

He smiled at her. 'You know, you really are a very nice person,' he said softly.

She wrinkled her nose. 'I'm not that nice,' she said, 'at least, not at the moment. I might be nicer once I've had a bath.'

He laughed softly, pulled open the door of the airing cupboard and threw her a towel. 'Here you are, go and have your bath. You know where the bathroom is.'

She soaked for ages, until all her skin had wrinkled on her fingers and the water had grown cool, and then she got out, dried herself and contemplated her dirty clothes. Just then there was a tap on the door.

'At the risk of losing any more of my wardrobe, I've put another pair of jeans and a shirt outside the door for you, and the coffee's done.'

She heard his soft footfall going down the hall, and opened the door to retrieve the clothes. The jeans were a little looser, probably because they were still in use, unlike the others, but the shirt was silk and felt like butter against her skin. Her bra was grubby and dusty from her day's work, so she'd bundled it up with her other clothes, and the fine fabric of the shirt teased her bare breasts like the warm touch of a lover.

She went along to the kitchen and found it in darkness, but she could hear soft music coming from the sitting room, and going in there she found Nick slumped on the sofa, his feet up on the low table, a cup of coffee propped on his belt buckle. He looked utterly relaxed and absolutely gorgeous, and as she went in he looked up and patted the cushion beside him, a welcoming smile in his eyes.

'Come and sit here,' he murmured.

It wasn't a hard decision to make. Helen settled herself beside him, and the arm which had been resting on the back of the sofa slipped down to circle her shoulders and ease her against him. With a contented sigh, she rested her head on his shoulder and allowed herself to relax.

'This is so nice,' she mumbled.

'Don't forget your coffee,' he reminded her, but she couldn't be bothered to move. She just lay there, like a boneless cat, and all but purred. She felt a chuckle rumble through his chest under her ear, and an involuntary smile played around her mouth.

Nick fed her chocolate mints, dipped in his coffee, and then he dropped one. It skidded down her chin and landed on his chest. She picked it up and ate it, and he wiped the shirt, but then he looked at her and put his coffee down. 'Come here,' he said gruffly. 'You've got chocolate on your chin.'

She held her chin towards him for him to wipe it, but he didn't wipe it—he leant forwards instead and licked the chocolate off with his tongue. Her eyes widened, and she saw the heat flare in his.

'Dammit, woman, you have the sexiest eyes,' he muttered, just before he took her mouth.

She whimpered and leant into him, and he turned

her beneath him on the sofa, shifting his weight so they lay full length along it, breast to chest, hip to hip, thigh to thigh.

His mouth devoured her, feasting eagerly on her lips, tracking over her throat and down over the silk to take her nipple in his mouth.

Because she wasn't wearing a bra she felt the heat instantly, and as his lips settled over the straining peak he groaned and lifted her up against his mouth, suckling her hungrily through the fine, soft fabric.

She cried out and bucked against him, and he left her nipple, lifting his head and staring down into her feverish eyes.

'Dear God, I want you,' he whispered tautly. 'Helen, stay with me. Spend the night here. Let me make love to you.'

Her whole body ached for him, her limbs trembled, and she had a burning need only he could fill.

Even so, from somewhere she found the strength to shake her head.

'No. I can't. Nick, please.'

'Why?'

She couldn't answer, because she couldn't say the words aloud.

She couldn't tell him why she mustn't stay—that it was because she loved him, and if she stayed with him, let him love her, let him fill her, then she'd be wide open to all that hurt again, and she'd promised herself she wouldn't be, not after Tony.

She'd thought she could indulge in an affair, but maybe she was wrong. Whatever, panic filled her, and she struggled to sit up.

'I just can't. Please—let me go.'

He didn't move for a moment, but then he shifted his weight, swinging his legs over the side of the sofa and standing up. He crossed to the window, standing rigidly with his back to her, frustration etched in every line of his body.

She knew all about that. Her own body was screaming with need, and the little bit of her that was pleading for common sense was almost drowned out by this wanton desire he'd awoken in her.

'I'll walk you back to your car,' he said tersely, and she stood up, tugging the damp silk away from her nipples, her feet searching blindly for her shoes.

She went out to the kitchen and scooped up her clothes, then paused in the doorway.

'I'm ready,' she said quietly, and with a sigh he turned towards her. His face was carefully expressionless, but his eyes were unable to disguise the frustration and need that stalked him.

It made her want to cry. She'd never meant this to happen, never wanted it, but she was aching too. She turned away, unable to look at him any more, and he fell into step beside her.

Nick walked her back to her car in the front garden of her cottage, but he didn't touch her again. He didn't trust himself. He watched her taillights disappear down the road, and then strode quickly down her garden, slotted the fence panel back into place and made his way back to his house.

The sitting room had no appeal for him. He gave the sofa a black look, collected up the coffee-cups—

hers untouched, as she'd left it—and threw the last of the chocolates into the bin. He didn't need any reminders of the cause of his frustration.

He went to bed, alone in the empty house, and lay for ages staring at the ceiling.

Frustration tortured him. He could easily have dealt with the physical manifestation of his need, but it was the emotional aspect that was like a twisting blade inside him, and nothing would alleviate that.

Nothing except Helen beside him. Under him. He rolled over, burying his face in the pillow, and fought down the tears of frustration and loneliness that rose up to swamp him.

He needed her.

Dear God, he loved her.

'Bloody fool,' he muttered, his voice clogged with tears. 'Whatever made you think you could talk her into it? You're just making an idiot of yourself.'

He tried to think about Sue. Her memory usually soothed him, but tonight he couldn't even picture her. She was lost to him, and he felt more alone than he had in the whole of the last five years.

A sob rose in his throat, and he pressed his fist against his mouth and held it back, but it wouldn't be held.

'Damn,' he whispered, and then the tears came, hot, scalding tears that washed away the frustration and left nothing behind but emptiness.

CHAPTER EIGHT

THE following morning the tension between the two of them could have been cut with a knife. They walked around each other as if they were treading on eggshells, and Julia, after a few abortive attempts at conversation, gave up and left them to it.

Lawrence was back, and Helen met him for the first time that morning. He was older than Nick, a little shorter, a little stouter, and his hair was thinning on top, but he had the kindest eyes that Helen had ever seen. She got the distinct feeling that they were also very good at divining her innermost secrets, so she vowed to avoid spending too much time with him.

Nick, however, wasn't able to indulge himself in that luxury. He had to hand over all the admin, and Lawrence, of course, took one look at him and realised something was seriously wrong.

'I think we'd better have a bit of a chat after surgery,' the older man suggested just before they started work. 'Go over a few things.'

'Good idea,' Nick agreed, hoping he'd be able to keep the conversation strictly to business, but, of course, Lawrence had known him far too long, and through far too much, to be fobbed off with any feeble attempt at subterfuge, and he didn't think for a moment he'd get away with it.

Still, he'd got a couple of hours' grace. Maybe he'd

think up something convincing to put him off the scent in that time.

Helen went into her consulting room, closed the door and sighed. Working with Nick under these conditions was going to be a nightmare. Still, at least they didn't have to work side by side. It was just the time between patients that was going to be awkward, and she could engineer her way around that if she was clever enough.

She pressed the button for her first patient, and for a while her surgery moved smoothly, all her appointments arriving on time and taking only the allotted number of minutes, by a miracle.

And then Mrs Hardy arrived and pulled out a sheet of paper.

'I don't see the doctor very often,' she said with an apologetic smile, 'so I've made a list.'

Helen sighed inwardly. She could see the list from where she was sitting, and it was numbered down the side from one to five.

Five, for heaven's sake! It would take half an hour to work her way through that lot, and it would totally throw her timekeeping for the rest of the morning. Still, she didn't have anything after her surgery, and it was better to be busy under the circumstances. God forbid she should have too much time to think!

'I tell you what, Mrs Hardy, why don't you read me your list, and then tell me in order of priority what you think is your most urgent problem? Then we'll see what we can get through. You might need to make another appointment for some of the things.'

Mrs Hardy looked slightly astonished. 'Oh, well, I thought it would save time, as I was here.'

'Well, it probably would,' Helen agreed, 'but I have eight patients an hour, so technically we've only got seven and a half minutes for your appointment. That's really not very long to deal with so many things.'

Her face fell. 'Oh, I see, I didn't realise. I thought I could just sort it all out at once.'

'Well, let's just have a look and see what we can deal with. Why don't you read me the list?'

So Mrs Hardy went through her list, starting with a problem that had brought her to the surgery that day, a persistent pain in her right foot when she walked.

'Have you twisted it? Or bought new shoes that put your feet into a different or unaccustomed position?'

'Ah, now I think about it, I have got some new shoes, a little bit higher than I usually wear.'

'OK, what's next?'

'Oh. Well, it's nothing much really, but I keep getting alternate bouts of diarrhoea and constipation from time to time, and it's just a bit wearing.'

Helen jotted that down, and looked up. 'Next?'

'My knees ache.'

'All the time, or just when you go up and downstairs, or if you walk a long way?'

'On the stairs, really,' she offered.

'And is that recent?'

Mrs Hardy shook her head. 'It's been getting worse for a couple of years.'

'What's next?'

'I feel tired all the time, but I've put on weight, so I expect that might be something to do with it, but I was a bit worried, with the bowel thing—and a cousin of mine had bowel cancer, so I'm a little bit wary.'

'I expect the tiredness and the knees and the weight gain are all connected,' Helen said, thinking aloud. 'So, what have we got? The foot, the tummy trouble, the knees, feeling tired, putting on weight?'

'That wasn't one of them.'

'So what's left?'

The middle-aged woman looked a little uncomfortable. 'Well, it's my husband who's suffering from this one,' she said with an embarrassed little laugh. 'I don't know, I just don't seem to be interested in our love life any longer. To be truthful, I find it all a little uncomfortable, especially afterwards, a couple of hours or so later. I get a really deep ache, right inside, and it just puts me off.'

'I can understand that,' Helen said sympathetically. 'Actually, Mrs Hardy, this all makes sense. I think what you have is an irritable bowel, which can give you pain on or after intercourse, constipation and diarrhoea alternately, and if it's caused by a food intolerance, such as wheat or dairy products, it can also affect your joints. So that would take care of the tummy, the knees, feeling tired, maybe putting on weight, and certainly the pain on intercourse.'

She smiled. 'Perhaps it's just as well you brought the list, because it's made it easier to track it down. Now, all we have to do is find out what's causing the problem, and avoid it. Then you should start to see an improvement.'

She scribbled on a few blood test forms and handed them to her. 'Right, I'd like you to see the practice nurse for some blood tests, to check for allergies and so on, and then I think the best thing to do is to make you an appointment with the dietician, and she can work on an exclusion diet with you. In the meantime, eat plenty of fruit and vegetables, lots of fibre, and ask your husband to be patient. I'm sure, if you're resourceful, you can find a way to avoid doing the things that hurt you without sacrificing too much of your fun.'

She sent Mrs Hardy off to make an appointment with the nurse and the dietician, apologised to her next few patients for the delay, and ended her surgery only twenty minutes late.

Nick dawdled through his surgery, hoping Lawrence would find himself something to do, but no such luck. Julia turned him straight round, and he found himself tucked up in Lawrence's room with a tray of coffee and biscuits and that avuncular gaze fixed firmly on him.

'How's your father?' Nick asked, in a vain attempt to sidetrack him.

'Not good. None of us are, really, but you just have to move on.' He stared at his coffee thoughtfully, and looked at Nick. 'So, how's it been without me? Young Dr Moore seems to have settled in well.'

There was a pregnant silence, and Nick was obliged to fill it. 'Yes, she's been excellent, she was a real find.'

'In more ways than one, I think,' Lawrence murmured, and Nick shifted uncomfortably in his chair.

This time he refused to fill the silence, because there was nothing he could say that wouldn't dump him in even hotter water.

'So that's how the land lies,' Lawrence said softly.

'Lawrence, butt out,' Nick told him with exaggerated politeness.

His partner chuckled. 'I wondered how long it would take for you to wake up again. You've been on ice for the last five years, and I've often wondered what kind of a woman it would take to bring you back to life.'

'I don't know what you're talking about,' Nick muttered. 'She's just a colleague.'

'And pigs fly,' he said mildly. 'I take it things aren't going smoothly in the land of hearts and flowers—has she got some kind of previous entanglement that's made her wary?'

Nick snorted. 'Apparently so. She thinks all men are bastards when it comes to love.' He didn't tell him the details—mostly because he didn't have them to give. Only that very scant outline that hinted of unimaginable pain and humiliation.

'So prove you're not.'

'I've tried, Lawrence,' he said wearily. 'I've done my damnedest, and every time I think I'm getting somewhere, she shuts down on me.'

'So don't give her time to think.'

Good advice, he thought, but hard to implement. He didn't think he'd given her much time to think last night, but apparently there'd been a chink of light that had broken through and blown it. He shook his head slowly.

'Can we talk about something else?' he asked gruffly, still too raw to want to revisit the scene of the crime, and for once Lawrence relented.

'Tell me all about the practice,' he said. 'Fill me in on what's been going on.'

So Nick told him about the problems that had afflicted his patients—that Mrs Emery had been to see Helen twice and she'd advised her to get a job, which caused Lawrence to chuckle, and that Mr Palmer had had a heart attack and Helen had had to deal with him.

'Does it still smell as bad out there?' Lawrence asked, and Nick gave a little huff of laughter.

'Apparently so. She doesn't think the sheets have been changed in years.'

Lawrence shook his head. 'Funny, isn't it? You get some people who scrub themselves with a scouring pad before they come to the doctor, and others that live in total squalor and don't seem to care or notice.'

He rubbed a hand over his chin and avoided Nick's eye. 'So, how's the admin been going? I gather from Julia you've been getting on really well with it—'

'Oh, no,' Nick said with a laugh, raising his hand to ward off the suggestion. 'You don't get out of it that easily! If you imagine you can skive off for a week or two and come back and find it's off your schedule for keeps, you've got another think coming. You're the senior partner, you deal with it.'

Lawrence snorted in disgust. 'You're a hard man, Nick Lancaster,' he said reproachfully.

They exchanged a smile, and then Nick got to his feet. 'I've got calls to make—and you've got some paperwork to attend to. Julia's got it all ready for you.'

He grinned mischievously and walked out, almost bumping into Helen in the hallway.

Immediately his body went into overdrive, and he dragged some much-needed air into his lungs and nodded a curt greeting before striding away down the corridor to the office. He picked up the notes, put on his jacket and was out of the door before Helen entered the room.

Nick was gone. She'd wanted a word with him, having spent the early part of the morning trying to avoid him but having come to the conclusion, somewhere in between Mrs Hardy and the end of her surgery, that it wouldn't work.

She needed to talk to him, to dispel the awful tension between them, to apologise for what she'd done the night before—or rather, hadn't done.

And now he was out, doing his rounds, and by the time he came back she'd be long gone, up to her elbows in paintbrushes and not-quite-white emulsion. Damn.

Helen changed into her oldest jeans, pushing aside the silk shirt that she'd worn last night with the little watermark over one nipple. Just looking at the faint stain made her body yearn, and she pulled out a T-shirt and slammed the drawer shut. The sooner she was moved into her own place and had a plentiful supply of her own clothes, the better. Then she wouldn't have to keep showering and changing at his house, and borrowing his clothes.

Not that it was likely to happen again, not after last night. He'd been so distant with her this morning that it seemed highly unlikely he'd ever talk to her again except when it was unavoidable and strictly business.

Still, it was what she wanted, wasn't it? No involvement?

Heartsick and exhausted from lack of sleep, she drove up to the cottage, let herself in and went upstairs. The bathroom door was open, and she could see the tiles that Nick had so patiently and carefully put on the walls just yesterday.

It seemed impossible that it had only been twenty-four hours ago. So much had happened, or not happened, and just looking at the tiles made her want to cry. They'd been getting on so well, but then suddenly their relationship had moved too fast and she'd panicked.

And why? Because she'd realised that she loved him? That was silly. There was no point in having a relationship with somebody she didn't like, and just because she loved him it didn't mean she couldn't have a relationship with him. She'd realised that, at some time in the middle of the night, when she'd been fidgeting about restlessly in her lonely bed. It didn't change anything, she still wasn't going to marry him or live with him, but it needn't change her plans for adopting a child. Lots of people had affairs and didn't live with anyone. Why not her? And with the gap in the fence at the end of the garden, they could be so discreet about it that no one would ever know.

Except, of course, that Nick wasn't talking to her this morning, and so all this speculation might be completely in vain.

She pulled on her new overalls, prised the lid off a tin of paint and started on the woodwork in her bedroom. By the time the light faded, she'd finished all of it, some of it with a second coat, and she was starving hungry.

She realised she'd been secretly hoping that Nick would pop in with his usual offer of supper but, of course, he hadn't. She hadn't really expected it, but it was only now when he hadn't come that she registered the feeling as disappointment.

She really didn't fancy another take-away, either Chinese or Indian, and she couldn't cope with fish and chips. She went back to the surgery, made herself a piece of toast and a cup of tea, showered and went to bed. At eleven her mobile phone rang, and she answered it warily.

It was Nick.

'Where are you?' he asked, and his voice sounded a little gruff and unused.

'At the surgery.'

'Can we talk?' he suggested. 'I've got Sam here, so I can't leave, but I'd really like to see you.'

'Now?' She hadn't told him she was in bed, but she wasn't in any danger of going to sleep, so it didn't really matter.

'I'm sorry, it's late. Forget it.'

'No, Nick—'

He'd hung up. She stared at the phone for a moment, then threw it in her bag, scrambled out of bed and pulled on her clothes. He wanted to talk to her, and she wanted to talk to him. There didn't seem to be any point in letting him put it off.

The kitchen light was still on when Helen arrived at his house, and she parked on the drive, with the car tucked round the corner out of sight of the street, and with her heart in her mouth she raised her hand to tap on the door. He opened it instantly, before she'd had a chance to knock, and his face was carefully expressionless. 'I didn't mean to keep you up,' he said quietly, but she shook her head.

'I wasn't asleep. Anyway, I wanted to talk to you, too.'

'Come on in. I was about to make hot chocolate. Do you fancy one?'

'Thanks,' she said, feeling suddenly awkward and unsure of her reception. But that was silly, because he'd phoned her, and now he was offering her a drink, so after all this he wasn't going to tell her to keep the hell out of his life.

At least, she hoped he wasn't, because she didn't think she'd be able to cope with that.

She followed him to the kitchen but, instead of sitting on the stool and making herself at home, stood awkwardly to one side with her arms wrapped round her waist, supporting herself before she fell over. Her heart was pounding, her palms felt damp and she thought she'd be sick with tension.

He turned with the mugs in his hand, took one look at her and put them down, then drew her into his arms.

'I'm sorry,' he mumbled against her hair. 'I don't

know what happened last night. I didn't mean to push you so hard.'

'It's OK,' she whispered, leaning against him and absorbing the hard warmth of his body, the tremors slowly leaving her as she absorbed his forgiveness as well as his warmth. 'I'm sorry, too. I shouldn't have run like that.'

'I gave you no choice.'

'That's rubbish. You gave me a perfectly good choice. I just panicked. I should have stayed.' She took a deep breath. 'I wish I had.'

He groaned quietly. 'Don't tell me that—not now, when Sam's here and there's nothing I can do about it.'

She smiled against his shirt. 'I'm sorry.'

'Don't apologise,' he ordered gruffly, tipping her chin with one blunt fingertip. It traced her mouth, glided up the line of her jaw, came back to outline her lips again.

She flicked her tongue out to moisten them, and his fingertip dragged slightly on the damp skin. She let her breath out on a ragged sigh, and his eyes darkened and he lowered his head to hers.

'You're so beautiful,' he sighed, his mouth whispering over hers, hardly making contact. 'I want you.'

'I know,' she said unsteadily. 'Nick, we can't.'

'I know. It's OK. Trust me.'

His hands cradled her face, and his kisses were gentle and undemanding.

They were no less arousing for that, and by the time he lifted his head her body was trembling and his was as taut as a bowstring. He wrapped her in his arms and eased her closer, and she felt the hard ridge of his arousal against her body.

He groaned, rocking against her, and she swallowed hard and struggled for air. It was impossible. Her breath kept jamming in her throat, and her body ached with need.

'I wonder if I can get a babysitter?' he said with a strangled laugh, and she smiled ruefully.

'Probably not—not one that won't tell the whole village what we're doing.'

'Right now, I couldn't care less,' he said gruffly, and hugged her hard before releasing her. 'Come on, let's drink this hot chocolate.'

Nick picked up the mugs and pulled a face. 'Did I say hot chocolate? Try tepid.'

He whirled them in the microwave for a moment, then they went through to the sitting room and sat on the sofa, their shoulders and thighs touching, and bit by bit the raging fire in her subsided.

It didn't go, not completely, but that was too much to expect, because it had never completely left her since she'd first met him two and a half weeks ago.

'How's the cottage coming on?' he asked, and Helen had an insane desire to laugh. He couldn't really be interested, she thought, but as a ploy to distract them from more fundamental issues it was probably as good as any other, so she played along with him.

'OK. I've nearly finished my bedroom, and the plaster's dry in the sitting room now so I can do that next, and I thought I'd get all my things that are in store delivered at the end of the week.'

'So you'll be in by the weekend?'

She nodded. 'I hope so. There's no point in trying to do it before then, because I'm just not ready, but I can spend the weekend unpacking.'

'Sam's going to Sue's parents for the weekend,' he said softly, and heat shimmered over her skin. 'I could help you.'

'When does he go?' she asked, trying not to sound too eager.

'Friday night. I'll take him over at about six—they live near Cambridge, so I won't be back until about nine.'

And then they'd have the whole weekend to themselves, she thought with heady anticipation.

It was Monday. That left Tuesday, Wednesday, Thursday and Friday to get through.

It was going to be a long week.

CHAPTER NINE

THE weekend seemed an awfully long way away. Helen contacted the removal firm and arranged to have all her furniture and boxes delivered at midday on Friday, and then the pressure was on.

She still had a great deal to do, so all her spare time that week was dedicated to working furiously on the house, partly to get it ready, and partly to give her something to do to take her mind off Nick and the coming weekend.

It didn't help, of course, that he came round in the evenings to 'help her paint', and ended up distracting her. Even when he did nothing, even when he really worked, just having him there nearly drove her crazy.

He had a pair of tatty old jeans and a ragged T-shirt with a rip in it that he wore for decorating, and because the rip was L-shaped the flap hung open, giving her a perfect view of his rippling back muscles as he moved. Several times she nearly tore it off him, but somehow she managed to restrain herself, often by taking herself off into another room and doing something completely different, just so she didn't have to look at him.

And every evening, she ended up eating either with him and Sam, or alone with him, picnicking cross-legged on the lawn in the middle of her garden.

As a refined form of torture, it was without equal.

She tried to concentrate at work but, having heard about the new doctor, a large number of her 'patients' had absolutely nothing wrong with them at all.

As far as the rest were concerned, most of them seemed to be women, relieved at last to have a female doctor. And amongst these, of course, were serious problems that had been neglected. Mrs Andrews, a woman in her early sixties, came to see her on Thursday morning, complaining of abdominal distension, bowel symptoms, pain on intercourse and, most worryingly, accompanying weight loss.

She said if she lay down and relaxed, she could feel a lump inside, and when Helen palpated her abdomen, she could feel a definite mass in the lower right quadrant. She gave her a pelvic examination, and something about the feel of the mass made her suspect either an ovarian cyst or an ovarian cancer.

That worried her. Ovarian cancer was the most common of all gynaecological cancers, the hardest to diagnose, and it had the poorest prognosis. On the other hand, ovarian cysts were common, had similar symptoms and would certainly present with a similar mass.

Whatever, Mrs Andrews needed urgent referral, and while Helen tried to play down the possible significance of the symptoms, she also had to make sure that Mrs Andrews was aware of the importance of following up this problem as quickly as possible.

'Do you think I have cancer?' the woman asked her frankly, and Helen had to admit that it was a possibility.

'I'm going to make an urgent referral, but if you

have private medical insurance, or if you would rather pay, you could see somebody sooner.'

'We have insurance, it's part of my husband's retirement package,' the woman said. 'What do we have to do to speed things up?'

'I can phone the consultant,' Helen told her. 'I'll have to send him a letter, but I can write that as soon as my surgery is finished, and you can collect it at twelve o'clock. You should be seen before the end of the week.'

She nodded. 'Thank you. I was going to come sooner, but I was afraid to. Now I wish I had, but I didn't want to see one of the men, not for something so personal. Isn't it silly? Now I know it's something so serious, or could be, that seems all so trivial.'

She seemed near to tears, and Helen asked her if she had come alone.

'No,' she said, shaking her head. 'My husband's in the waiting room.'

'Do you want me to talk to him?'

She shook her head again. 'No, it's all right, I won't worry him yet. I'll see the consultant first.'

'Well, if you don't get an appointment very quickly, do come back to me, won't you? And if there's anything else you want to ask in the meantime, please, ring or come back.'

Helen watched her go, mentally crossing her fingers that it was a simple cyst and nothing more sinister.

As she put the finishing touches to her dining-room that afternoon, she thought about Mrs Andrews and how she'd been reluctant to see a male doctor. She could understand it, of course, and as Mrs Andrews herself pointed out, it was something that she now regretted.

She told Nick about it when he arrived at six-thirty, and he rolled his eyes and groaned. 'That's so silly,' he said heavily. 'I'm just a doctor, she's just another woman like every other one. Why won't they come?'

'Because it's very personal, and they feel embarrassed. How would you feel coming to see me if you thought you had testicular cancer?'

'More worried about cancer than my modesty,' he said pragmatically.

'How about sexual dysfunction?'

He laughed softly. 'I'd rather see a woman— they're kinder, and you don't have to keep up an image with a woman. Anyway, there's no danger of that, not at the moment. I think my system's in hyper-drive.'

Helen felt soft colour flood her cheeks, and with a ragged laugh he pulled her into his arms. 'One more day,' he murmured. 'Just hang on in there, it's nearly over.'

He kissed her, and she felt the now-familiar longing leap to life. Tomorrow, she thought. I've only got to wait until tomorrow, and we can be alone together without worrying about Sam.

Just then they heard footsteps running down the path, and they broke apart guiltily just as Sam and Tommy burst into the kitchen. 'Dad, we've had the wickedest idea! How about if Grandma and Grandpa come here instead of me going to them? Then they can see my tree-house!'

Nick cleared his throat and avoided looking at Helen.

'Um, I doubt if they'll want to come all this way just to see your tree-house, Sam,' he pointed out, but Sam was irrepressible.

'They could come for the weekend!' he suggested.

Helen thought Nick was going to choke.

'But they're expecting you there. They will have bought all sorts of goodies to feed you on—you know what they're like. Maybe another weekend, son,' he said, and Helen wondered if Sam could hear the slightly desperate tone in his father's voice.

She had a terrible urge to giggle, and she had to take herself out of the room and busy herself with some trivial task until she had herself under control again.

She could hear Nick reasoning with Sam, and also pointing out that before he burst into her house, it might be polite to knock.

'Sorry,' Sam mumbled, clearly crushed by his father's lack of enthusiasm for his brilliant idea. 'Come on, Tommy, let's go back to the tree-house.'

Helen listened to them go, then went back to the kitchen just as Nick turned to her, the laughter bubbling up in him. 'I didn't know if I was going to get away with that one,' he said with a wry shake of his head.

'It was a little close for comfort,' she said with a smile. 'I wondered how you were going to get out of it.'

'*You* wondered?' He rolled his eyes. 'Anyway, I very much doubt if they could have got here for the weekend, because they've got dogs and cats and they're all elderly now and can't be left in kennels, and it takes them weeks to arrange any time away.'

'Thank heavens for small mercies,' Helen said with a grin. 'Anyway, enough of that. Help me with this kitchen. What on earth am I going to do with it?'

He looked around it and scrubbed his chin thoughtfully, and the rasp of his stubble against his hand was curiously arousing. She wanted to touch it, to feel the rough scrape of the coarse hairs against her palm, to feel them graze her body as his mouth trailed over it, feeding hungrily on her—

'Helen?'

She flushed, so caught up in her thoughts she hadn't heard a word he'd said. 'Sorry, I was miles away.'

His smile was wry with understanding. 'Hell, isn't it?'

And there were still twenty-four hours to go.

Her furniture arrived on the dot of twelve, just moments after she got to the cottage, and she spent the next two hours trying to remember what was in each box and getting them put somewhere suitable.

She didn't have any carpets yet, of course, and the local firm hadn't been able to arrange it until the following week, so in the end she had them stack all the downstairs stuff in the dining-room and all the upstairs stuff in the spare bedroom.

Only the furniture was put into the right rooms, and it looked sparse and barely adequate. Still, once the pictures were up it would be different.

The men left, and she wandered round her house, hugging herself and trying to imagine what it would be like once the curtains were up, the carpets were down and pictures were on the walls.

Wonderful. She could hardly wait, but it didn't make sense to unpack anything properly until the carpets were down. In any case, she knew she'd be spending most of the weekend with Nick.

She found some sheets and made her bed, unpacked the curtains and held them up at the window. They were very creased, a little bit short and too wide, but they would do for now. She hooked them up onto the old rail, stood back and looked at them. Well, they'd give her a little privacy until they could be replaced, and that was the best that could be said for them.

'Kitchen,' she said firmly, and went downstairs and unpacked all the pots and pans, her kettle, the washing-up bowl, her plates and mugs and cutlery—all her familiar bits and pieces that she needed to hand so that she could actually cook proper meals at home, instead of going to the pub or all the take-aways in the village. It was going to be bliss. Much healthier, much cheaper, and a much wider choice. And because she was only working part time, she'd have the energy and enthusiasm to be a little inventive.

She looked at her watch, and her pulse speeded up. It was seven o'clock. Nick would be at Cambridge by now, and in two hours he would be back with her. And there was no way she'd be ready!

She shut the windows, locked up the cottage and drove down to the surgery, throwing all her things into the car higgledy-piggledy and driving quickly back to the cottage. She brought all her things into the house, hung up the clothes in her wardrobe, opened a large suitcase that had been in store and rummaged through it for her favourite dress.

She'd hardly worn it before because she hadn't really had any occasion to do so, but she was going to wear it tonight. She hung it up on the front of the wardrobe for the creases to fall out, and went and ran her first bath in her new bathroom.

She washed her hair, then piled it up on her head and squirted a dollop of bubble bath into the water, swishing it round with her fingers until it made a thick foam. Then she slid down in the water and sighing with relish, she relaxed for the next half-hour.

The following thirty minutes were spent on all the exclusively female preparations that a woman makes when she knows her body is going to be the subject of intimate attention. By the time she'd finished, her skin was smooth and silky and she felt pampered and beautiful. She'd even put nail varnish on her toenails.

She found her best underwear, pulled on her dressing-gown over it and took the dress down to the kitchen. It was wonderful to have her iron and ironing-board back, and she ran the iron quickly over the dress to refresh it before slipping it on.

She looked in the mirror on the front of her wardrobe, and smiled with satisfaction. She looked good, she knew she did. She'd deliberately kept her make-up simple, her hair was shining with health, swinging loose around her shoulders, and the soft, sandwashed silk dress clung gently to her every curve.

It was a beautiful colour, a soft greenish gold, not a colour everyone could wear but wonderful with her ash blonde hair and her muddy green eyes. She put a simple gold chain around her neck, a matching one on her wrist, and slipped her feet into a pair of plain low court shoes.

All she needed now was Nick.

The drive back was filled with nail-biting tension. Nick felt ridiculously nervous, racked with stage fright and obsessed with a fear of failure. As he turned into the village, his heart started to pound.

What if he couldn't please Helen? What if, after all this time, he'd forgotten how a woman's body worked?

'You're being ridiculous,' he told himself. 'Of course you haven't forgotten. The worst that's going to happen is that you'll blow it.'

He pulled up outside the house, ran in and showered, threw his dirty clothes in the laundry basket and ran a hasty eye over his bedroom. The bed was made up with clean sheets, the curtains were closed, the lamps were lit.

The scene was set.

God, he was nervous. He closed his eyes and drew a few steadying breaths, then slowly, calmly, he walked out of the house, locked the door behind him and drove round to Helen's cottage. The lights were on, and for the first time he rang the front doorbell and stood back, his hands rammed into his pockets, waiting for her to open the door.

He didn't have long to wait. It swung open, and

she stood there, backlit by the harsh, bare bulb, her hair like a halo around her head. She stepped back a little and smiled, and his heart missed a beat. She looked stunning.

'Do you want to come in? I'm ready, I just have to pick up my bag and a cardigan in case I get cold later.'

He shook his head. 'No. I'll wait for you.'

She was gone only a couple of seconds, and then she was there, an uncertain smile playing around her lips.

She's nervous, he thought in amazement, and suddenly he felt better. He opened the car door for her and settled her in, then went round and slid behind the wheel. It took less than a minute to drive to his house, and finally he was ushering her in. The door closed behind them and she turned to him with a shy smile. He cupped her shoulders in his hands and drew her against him, lowering his mouth to feather a kiss against her lips.

That was all it took. Like a spark on tinder, the fire caught hold and within moments it was raging.

With a ragged groan he took her mouth, plundering it hungrily, and she whimpered and pressed herself against him. He'd meant to take it slowly, to woo her, to be gentle with her, but there was nothing gentle about this. With almost savage thoroughness, he took her mouth again and again, and it was no longer enough.

He scooped her up in his arms, their mouths still locked together, and carried her down the corridor to his bedroom, kicking the door shut behind him. Then he lowered her to her feet, sliding her down his body so that she felt every intimate inch of it against her own.

Reluctantly he released her, standing back just far enough to turn her in front of him and unzip the dress. He eased it off her shoulders and it puddled to the floor at her feet, leaving her standing there in nothing but a few scraps of underwear.

He had a vague realisation that it was quite pretty underwear, but all he could think of was that he wanted to get rid of it, because it was in his way. His fingers shook as he unfastened the bra, but then the catch gave and her breasts spilled into his hands. He closed his eyes and groaned, then he slid his hands down and caught the top edge of the gossamer triangle of lace that passed for knickers, stripping them away.

He stepped back, raking his eyes over her, and he thought he must have died and gone to heaven.

'Have I ever told you you're beautiful?' he said roughly.

Her smile was a little unsteady, and he could see a soft wash of colour over her cheeks.

My God, she's shy, he thought, and it amazed him.

'Your turn,' she whispered, and he tried to unbutton his shirt, but his fingers were shaking so badly he could hardly do it. In the end he ripped it off, buttons pinging across the room, and kicked his shoes off one after the other. Unzipping his trousers, he hooked his thumbs into the waistband, catching his underpants as well and stripping them off in one.

Then they stood there face to face, eyes locked on

each other's, and the tension was unbearable. She cracked first, her eyes closing, a tiny pulse jumping in her throat.

'Nick?'

'What is it, sweetheart?' he asked unsteadily. 'Tell me what you want.'

'Hold me,' she begged.

With a harsh cry he gathered her up against his chest, and then his mouth found hers and meshed with it, and it was like coming home.

He lifted her onto the bed, laying her down in the middle of it and coming down beside her. A tremor ran through her, and she looked up at him and smiled shakily.

'Make love to me, Nick,' she whispered, and he closed his eyes for a moment and counted to ten.

He was going to lose it. He knew he was, just the moment he touched her. He reached out a trembling hand, running it lightly over her breast. So soft, so ripe, so unbelievably beautiful. The nipple puckered, peaking to his touch, and he bent his head and took it in his mouth. She arched up with a little cry, and he slid his hand down over her hip and pulled her against him, against the unimaginable ache. Her hands threaded through his hair, and she trapped his head against her, holding him. He turned his head and bit her wrist, just gently, and she cried out.

Strange, how he knew exactly how to touch her, where to touch her. His hand slid down and round, stroking the soft skin of her inner thigh, teasing the soft nest of curls, testing them. She cried out again, and he lifted his head and looked down at her.

'Please, Nick,' she begged in a ragged whisper.

He was unable to resist her any longer. Pausing only long enough to protect her from pregnancy, he entered her with one swift thrust. She cried out, arching up to meet him, her body strung taut like a bow. As he drove into her he felt the first ripples of her release, and with a broken cry he joined her, hurling himself over the precipice to freefall gently back to earth with her in his arms.

Hot tears scalded his eyes. Dear God, he'd forgotten, if he'd ever known, just how wonderful it felt. He swallowed hard, cradling her against his chest, and he felt a shudder run through her.

'Nick?'

'It's all right, my darling, I've got you.' His hands soothed her, stroking rhythmically over the soft skin of her back, tracing the hollow of her spine and the smooth curve of her hip. He could feel her tears against his shoulder, feel the shock waves still echoing through her, and he knew that she was just as stunned as he was.

He lifted his head and looked down at her, and saw the twin tracks of the tears down her cheeks. 'Oh, my love,' he sighed. 'Are you all right?'

She met his eyes, her own still sparkling with tears, and lifting a hand she laid it gently against his cheek.

'I didn't know,' she said quietly. 'I had no idea.'

He bent his head and kissed her, a gentle, reverent kiss, utterly different from the wild meshing of their mouths such a short time ago, and then he smiled down at her a little crookedly. 'Did I tell you how beautiful you look tonight?'

Unbelievably, Helen blushed, and he laughed softly at her. 'You really have no idea just how lovely you are, do you?' he murmured.

'Don't,' she said. 'Don't talk, Nick. Just hold me.'

He did. He moved them both under the covers, wrapped her in his arms and held her all night. They made love again and again, and in the middle of the night he made a sortie to the kitchen and returned with a tray full of nibbles and a bottle of sparkling wine.

The bubbles made her giggle, tickling her nose, and he took the glass away from her and fed her tasty little morsels, all carefully chosen aphrodisiacs—not that either of them needed them. He couldn't take his eyes off her, and every time she smiled at him, it was as if the sun had come out.

Finally, replete at last, they fell asleep a little before dawn, still wrapped in each other's arms.

Helen woke when a stray sunbeam found its way through a chink in the curtains and crept across the pillow to her face. Nick was still sleeping, one arm thrown up above his head, sprawled on his back in an attitude of total relaxation.

She smiled contentedly and sat up, wrapping her arms around her knees and looking around her. They must be in the base of the old post mill, she realised, because the room was circular. She hadn't noticed it before, because she'd had better things to think about, but as she looked around her now she thought what a wonderful room it was.

The walls were bare brick, the ceiling vaulted and

high, arching up into the roof, and beams spanned it at ceiling height. The furniture was simple, typical of Nick, an old country pine chest, a heavy wooden blanket box, a beautiful wardrobe with carved panels, made of satinwood. The windows in the room were small and spaced out, breaking the walls up into short sections that were difficult to furnish, and the sparseness gave it a simple, monastic quality.

She leant her head back against the heavy wooden headboard and looked down at him. There was nothing monastic about him. She didn't know how a man with his appetites had survived the last five years, but he had spent most of the last night making up for it.

And as for her, she'd learned things about her body she hadn't even dreamed of.

She hugged her knees, smiling as she remembered, blushing a little at the memories. She bent over and brushed her lips lightly over his forehead, and his eyes fluttered open.

A smile crinkled his eyes, and he rolled towards her and pulled her into his arms.

'Morning, gorgeous,' he said, his voice gruff with sleep. 'Sleep well?'

'Mmm, wonderful. You?'

'Bliss.' He pulled her closer, tangling his legs with hers, his body eager for her yet again. However, he did nothing, just lay there and held her, and she snuggled closer and wondered how it was possible to feel any happier.

'Have I told you just how much I love you?' he said quietly.

She lay very still, her breath caught in her throat.

Don't spoil it, she thought, don't make it complicated, please.

But he didn't hear her.

He lifted a hand and brushed the hair from her face, then stared deep into her eyes. 'Marry me, Helen,' he said softly. 'Share your life with me, help me bring up Sam, have babies with me. We'd make a wonderful family, you and me and Sam and all our babies.'

He was still watching her, his eyes, so full of love and tenderness, searching her face for her response.

For one almost believable moment, she was tempted to say yes, to agree to being a part of his life, to being a mother to Sam—beautiful, motherless Sam who needed a loving woman in his life—and a wife to Nick, who needed a woman, too, the woman he made her feel. She hovered, and then with sickening clarity she remembered all the reasons why she couldn't do this, why it was all just a dream. She felt frozen, her world tumbling down around her.

He wasn't supposed to feel like this, wasn't supposed to fall in love with her and want to marry her. She couldn't compete with Sue, couldn't fight with a ghost, and he was crazy to imagine that she would try. Besides, she had her own ghosts, and they were taunting her now, torturing her.

'I can't.'

Her voice was quiet, but in the breathless silence it sounded like the clash of cymbals.

A fleeting frown crossed his face, his eyes puzzled. 'What do you mean, you can't? Why not?'

'You know why not, Nick. I've told you. I'm never getting married, never getting involved in a long-term relationship. You knew that. I've told you my plans, and this doesn't change them. Just because you love me isn't enough. It can never be enough. I can't do it, I'm too afraid, there's too much to lose.'

He rolled to his back, staring up at the ceiling with sightless eyes, and when he turned back to her they were raw with pain.

'It's him, isn't it?' he said in a voice harsh with emotion. 'Well, I'm not your bloody Tony. You know that. This is me—Nick—and I love you.'

She closed her eyes, unable to bear the pain she could see on his face.

'I'm sorry,' she whispered unevenly.

'Sorry? I don't want you to be sorry, for God's sake! You love me, I know you do, but you can't marry me, because it's not enough? What the hell does it take? What more is there? What more can there be?'

She squeezed her eyes shut against the tears, but they leaked past, scalding her cheeks.

'I'm sorry,' she said again brokenly, her voice clogged with emotion.

She heard him get up, heard him moving around, opening drawers, shutting them, then the harsh click of the door closing behind him.

The sound nearly broke her heart. It would have done, if it hadn't been broken already. Instead, the cracks just opened up again, revealing the torn and damaged core, the unhealed wounds, the fear.

Tony had hurt her, promised her the world, and it had all been a lie. Was this a lie, too? She didn't think so, but what if it was? What if Nick realised after a while that he didn't really love her at all? What if it was just lust, and the memory of Sue got in the way and killed his feelings for her?

She hugged her arms around her shoulders and rocked herself gently in the middle of Nick's bed.

If only she could let herself love him—because he was right, of course, she did love him, but it wasn't enough, because she couldn't trust him, couldn't trust any man.

Not now, not again, not after Tony.

He's different, an inner voice echoed, but he wasn't. He was still a man, and if he met another woman a few years down the line, she could be another Jan, another woman like her own mother, another cheated wife.

She couldn't stand that.

Stiffly, her body shocked and exhausted by emotion, she climbed off the bed and dragged on her clothes. She'd go home. That was it. She'd go home, to her cottage, and lick her wounds. With any luck she could slip out past Nick without seeing him, and she wouldn't have to drag it all out and talk it through until her emotions were under control.

It might only take about four more years.

CHAPTER TEN

IT WAS the worst weekend of Helen's life. She'd thought she'd known unhappiness in the past, but it had been nothing like this.

She didn't see Nick again. He must have put on his clothes and left, because when she came out of the house, his car was gone and she was alone. Trembling violently with reaction, she scribbled him a note and put it by the kettle where she knew he'd find it, then she let herself out and went back to her cottage, struggling with the fence panel rather than walk round on the road in full view of everyone.

She let herself in, made a cup of tea and took it up to bed before the tears came, and then she rolled into the pillows and sobbed as though her heart were breaking.

Not surprising, really, since it was.

She felt devastated by loss, grief-stricken, be-reaved.

It was crazy. He wasn't dead, he was alive and well and had gone off to lick his wounds, she told herself, but she knew that what they'd had, that amazing, in-credible, beautiful loving they'd shared, was gone for ever, broken into a million pieces by a few carefully chosen words.

It just proved to her what she already knew, that she couldn't afford to allow herself to become so emotionally dependent upon somebody, because when it went wrong, as it inevitably would, her world would be devastated.

And once she had a child, she couldn't allow that to happen. She would have to be the rock on which the child depended, and she couldn't do that if she was falling apart inside.

She slept fitfully until midday, then got up and attacked all her boxes. She found a hammer and nails, unpacked all her pictures and put them up.

She found the rest of her curtains, but none of them really fitted, so she drove down to Ipswich, went into the nearest department store and bought herself some ready-made curtains in a plain cream damask for the sitting room, and two pairs of pretty, cottage curtains for the bedrooms. She didn't worry about the dining-room, she couldn't be bothered with that, and by the time she'd chosen the others she was overwhelmed again with the need to cry.

She went back to the car, drove out into the countryside and howled again. Then she pulled herself together, blew her nose, wiped her eyes and drove back to the cottage.

As she went past Nick's drive, she noticed that his car was back and her heart wrenched.

He didn't want to see her. It was pointless going round because she'd said all she needed to say, all there really was to say. Instead, she went home, unpacked and ironed her new curtains, and hung them up. She needed new tracks, really, but putting them up was beyond her, so she would have to wait until she could get a handyman.

One thing was for sure, it wouldn't be Nick.

She went to the village shop and bought herself a few basic provisions, went home and made scrambled eggs on toast, and realised it was the first thing she'd had to eat since the middle of the night, when Nick had fed her slivers of avocado and tasty morsels of chicken and fresh, juicy strawberries.

Remembering it made her cry again, tears welling up and spilling down her cheeks in endless rivers that dripped into her supper until she dashed them away angrily with the backs of her hands.

She made herself eat the eggs, even though she wasn't hungry, and then she went to bed again.

She didn't sleep. Although she was exhausted with emotion and lack of sleep from the night before, still it eluded her. The bed was too big, too empty without him, and she realised that it probably always would be.

She got up early on Sunday morning, dressed in jeans and boots and went out for a walk. She drove the car to a nearby heath, parked it and walked for hours, wandering aimlessly round in circles until she eventually found the car again.

She was too exhausted to cry now, too wrung out to feel anything. She went home, had a bath, surrounded by Nick's tiling, and went to bed. This time she did sleep, but her dreams were nightmares and she was only too ready to go to work on Monday morning.

Of course, the surgery was the last place she really wanted to be, because inevitably she would see Nick, but it had to happen, and she might as well get it over with. He wasn't there when she arrived, so she put on a brave face, smiled at Julia, made herself a cup of tea and took it into her consulting room, hiding there until the start of the surgery.

There was no way he'd come and find her there, she was sure he would avoid her, and so she felt relatively safe. However, she was tense, and every knock made her heart pound.

She had a phone call from Mr Hardy at eleven o'clock, just as she finished her surgery, to tell her that his wife had had her ovary removed and that the lump had been a benign cyst.

He sounded hugely relieved and almost pathetically grateful for Helen's help, and she thought, He loves her, he really loves her. What would he have done if she'd died?

How could anybody live their life drenched in so much emotion? It terrified her, all that love and need and dependence. She couldn't cope with it. She only needed to depend on herself, because nothing else could be relied on as permanent.

Helen cradled the phone after wishing Mrs Hardy well, picked up the notes and her mug, dragged in a deep breath and went out to the office. Nick was there, his back to her, and as she went in, he left, bag in hand.

Lawrence gave her an old-fashioned look, stood up and propelled her gently into the kitchen, closing the door firmly behind them.

'Cup of coffee?' he offered, and she nodded warily. She needed to be wary. Lawrence put the coffee down on the table, sat down opposite her and met her eyes searchingly.

'I don't suppose you'd like to tell me what's going on, would you? I can't get any sense out of Nick this morning, but you both look like hell and one of you must know what's going on.'

'If Nick wants you to know, then I expect he'll tell you,' she said, hanging on by a thread.

Lawrence snorted. 'That'll be the day. Nick never talks about anything. I've spent the last five years with my fingers crossed, hoping he'd survive, and finally I thought he was getting somewhere. Then this morning he walks in looking as if he's been hit by a truck, and we're back to square one.'

He stirred his coffee idly, giving her time, but she remained silent.

'I don't suppose you'd care to enlighten me, would you? You see, the thing is, I happen to be rather fond of the poor bastard, and I don't like to see anything happen to him.'

'He asked me to marry him,' she said unevenly.

'And I take it you said no?'

She nodded miserably. 'He wasn't meant to fall in love with me. I thought he just wanted an affair, I never realised how seriously he was taking it.'

'No, well, you wouldn't, because he never shares his feelings.'

'He did on Friday night,' she said quietly. 'I was just too blind to see it coming until it was too late.'

'And is this going to affect your position here?' Lawrence asked pragmatically, and she gave a helpless shrug.

'I don't know. Probably. He won't look at me, I can't talk to him, I don't know what to do—' She broke off, biting her lip against the tears, but they came anyway, and Lawrence just sat back quietly and let her cry.

'I'm sorry,' she said eventually. 'I thought I'd finished doing that.'

'Unlikely,' Lawrence scolded her gently. 'When you love somebody that much, you can cry for ever.'

Helen looked up at him with wide, tear-washed eyes, and shook her head. 'I don't...'

Lawrence just looked at her, his eyes filled with understanding, and she looked away, because the truth was reflected there in his eyes, and she couldn't bear to see it.

She stood up, scraping her chair back across the floor with a hideous noise, and backed towards the door. 'I have to go,' she said desperately, and turned and fled.

There was nothing more she could do at home until the carpets came, and she couldn't bear to go out in the garden, so close to Nick's, even though she knew he was at work. She got in the car and drove for hours, and then ran out of petrol and had to walk two miles, buy a can and walk back with it banging against her legs with every step.

Her feet hurt, because she was wearing her work shoes still, and she wanted to cry with pain and frustration and unhappiness, but she wouldn't let herself. She was finished crying, whatever Lawrence thought. She was tougher than that.

Almost.

*   *   *

Nick thought he knew all about pain, but over the next few days, he discovered he was wrong. He got through the days, somehow, but the evenings were the hardest, pretending to Sam that everything was all right when his world was falling apart.

And then at night, he had to go into his bedroom and lie in the bed where he'd shared his soul with Helen, and pretend to sleep.

He couldn't do it, any more than he could lie on the sofa in the sitting room and sleep, and he ended up moving into the spare bedroom and pretending to Sam that there was something wrong with the walls in his bedroom and he'd have to fix them before he could sleep in there again. It was a feeble lie, and he couldn't believe that Sam swallowed it, but of course he did, because Nick never lied to him.

Well, not until now, anyway.

He couldn't bear to go down the garden, but he did go down there once, with a hammer and some nails, and fixed the fence panel back permanently. He didn't look at Helen's cottage. He couldn't bring himself to, and he found himself wondering if all this would have happened if she hadn't bought it, and he hadn't spent so much time with her, helping her fix it up. If it had been anywhere else, he wouldn't have been able to help so much, because of Sam, but because he'd been able to keep an eye on him through the fence, it hadn't been a problem.

Well, it was a problem now.

It wasn't his only problem, though, by a long way. Whereas the cottage at the end of the garden just stayed there and minded its own business, the same couldn't be said of Lawrence. He meddled, he interfered and he nearly drove Nick crazy.

Nick knew what Lawrence was doing, of course. He was trying to break him down, make him talk about it, get it out in the open and deal with it. Sue would have done the same, of course, but Nick couldn't. It was too private, too deeply personal to share. His only comfort was that Helen, too, looked as bad as he felt.

He didn't know why that was a comfort. He didn't want her to be hurting. Fool that he was, he loved her too much to wish any pain on her.

Fortunately they were busy at work, and he threw himself into the practice with enthusiasm. He even took over some of the admin from Lawrence, but then Lawrence took it back because he was making such a mess of it. He was all right with the patients, but the admin couldn't really hold his attention, for all that he tried to make it.

He stole one of Lawrence's clinics, though, and did all the house calls.

On Thursday, he went to see Mr Palmer, who was home from hospital after his heart attack and still complaining of chest pain. Nick drove up to the farm, ran the gauntlet of the dogs and the malevolent son and stomped his way up to the bedroom.

'Oh, it's you, is it? Thought I'd get that young floozy again.'

Nick glared at him. 'Dr Moore's busy,' he told him bluntly. 'I gather you've still got chest pain?'

'Just a bit. Told the boy not to bother to get you, but he's stubborn, just like his mother.'

Nick grunted and got out his stethoscope, listened to his patient's chest, sounded it and listened to his heart. The beat was irregular, and he seemed to be suffering from atrial fibrillation. That was potentially dangerous, because clots could form in the heart and then get sent out to cause havoc in the rest of the body. 'Are you taking your warfarin regularly?' he asked.

'Rat poison? You got to be joking! No way I'm taking that. You're trying to kill me, all of you!'

'We're trying to keep you alive,' Nick explained patiently. 'It's to thin your blood, so you don't get clots in your heart muscle or your brain or your chest, so you don't have a heart attack or a stroke or a pulmonary embolus.'

The last was too much for him. He'd had a heart attack, he knew about strokes, but a pulmonary embolus was unheard of and a step too far for Mr Palmer.

'You're just trying to put the fear of God into me, aren't you?' he said angrily. 'Go on, get out of here. I don't need your help, you quack.'

Nick shut his bag with a defiant snap and picked it up. 'Call me what you like,' he said, 'but if you don't take your warfarin, you're very likely to die. It's up to you. I can only tell you the facts.'

He went downstairs and left the foetid cottage, dragged in a lungful of pure, clean air and went and found the son.

'He's not too bad,' Nick told him, 'but he must

take his pills regularly. Try and make sure he does, please, or I can't be responsible for what happens to him.'

The son grunted, and not for the first time Nick wondered if he was quite all right or if there was something slightly askew in his head.

With a mental shrug, he got back into the car and drove off, nearly running over one of the scruffy collies that attacked his wheels as he left. Oh, well, he thought, if the old man took his pills, maybe he wouldn't have to go out there again and visit him.

No such luck. The following morning at eight o'clock, just as he arrived at the surgery, there was a phone call to say that Mr Palmer had collapsed.

'Oh, damn, I'll go out and see him. I know what it is. He's been refusing to take his warfarin—said he wasn't having rat poison, silly old fool.' He turned to Lawrence. 'Can you sort out my patients, split them with you and Helen or something? I'll be back as soon as I can.'

He drove out to the farm as fast as he could, and as he arrived the son came out of the house, brandishing his gun.

'You killed him, you bastard!' he screamed. 'It's all your fault, round here yesterday, meddling in his pills. I made him take them last night, and now look what's happened! He's dead!'

With a sobbing cry, he raised the gun, pointed it at Nick and pulled the trigger.

'Nick not back yet?' Lawrence asked Julia after surgery had finished.

'No, there's been no word from him. Actually, I'm a little bit worried. I tried to ring the house, and his mobile, but I couldn't get any reply.'

Helen looked at them both. 'Where is he? I know he went out on a call, but that's all I know.'

'He's gone to see Mr Palmer,' Lawrence told her. He frowned, glanced at his watch and met Julia's eyes. 'I think I'll just run out there and check everything's OK.'

Helen felt panic rise in her chest. 'Try the phone again,' she suggested to Julia after Lawrence had gone.

She did, but again there was no reply.

'Lawrence will be there in five minutes, and he'll ring us. Don't worry. I expect what's happened is that he's left the farm and his car's broken down, and his phone is out of range. He'll be all right.'

Helen knew Julia was right, but all she could see was the man with the gun and her heart was filled with fear for Nick.

Ten minutes later, the phone rang. Julia answered it, and her face went white and she laid her hand across her chest. 'Yes, of course, I'll get her now.' She held the phone out to Helen with a trembling hand. 'It's Lawrence.'

Helen snatched the phone from Julia's hand. 'Hello?'

'I've found him, Helen,' Lawrence said urgently. 'He was at the farm. I've called an ambulance, and they're taking him to Ipswich hospital. I'm afraid he's been shot.'

'Shot?' she said, sitting down abruptly. 'Oh, my God, is he dead?'

'No, he's not dead, but I think you should go to the hospital.'

Panic swamped her. She grabbed her keys and ran to her car, breaking every speed limit on her way to the hospital.

She was there when the ambulance pulled up and they unloaded Nick, strapped to a stretcher and covered in blood-soaked bandages, with an oxygen mask on and saline drip running in. She got in the way, of course, and they tried to remove her from the scene, but she refused to be taken.

She shrugged them aside angrily, grabbing his hand and hanging onto it as if it was the only thing between him and death.

'Don't die, Nick, please, God, don't die—'

'I don't think he's going to die, unless it's because we can't get to him,' a doctor told her gently but firmly. 'He's quite stable, but he's lost a lot of blood and we need to have a proper look at him. Now, please, could you wait outside?'

Helen stood her ground. 'I'm a doctor,' she told them firmly, 'and I'm not going anywhere. I'll just stand here out of the way if you like, but there's no way I'm leaving, so don't even bother to suggest it.'

And so she propped up the wall, her arms wrapped firmly round her waist, and watched as they peeled away Nick's clothes and revealed his injuries. His left shoulder and arm were covered in tiny holes where the shot had penetrated, and there were one or two on the side of his face and head. He was peppered with them, but what she didn't know, and what they didn't know, was if any of them had penetrated vital organs.

The portable X-ray machine was wheeled in and they took plates of his head, and chest and arm. They were developed within moments, and put up on the light box in the corner of Resus.

'Well, at least they look superficial,' the doctor said with a sigh of relief. 'He'll have to go up to Theatre to have them removed, because there are so many of them, but I'm more worried about his head injury.'

'He's coming round,' one of the nurses said.

Helen spun round, hurrying to Nick's side as his eyes flickered open and struggled to focus.

'Nick?'

'Helen?' He looked around him, closed his eyes and groaned. 'That bastard shot me, didn't he?' he muttered.

'Looks like it. We're going to have to take you up to Theatre and get the shot out of you, but there doesn't seem to have been any serious damage. I think the police are waiting to talk to you, though,' the doctor told him.

He looked round for Helen, his eyes locking on her face when he found it, and his hand reached blindly out to her.

She took it, folding it against her chest and bending her head to press her lips against his fingers. 'Thank God you're all right,' she said fervently. She started to shake, the reaction setting in now she knew he would live. She squeezed her eyes shut, then opened them again and found him still looking at her with a strange intensity.

'Why are you here?' he asked.

'Because I love you,' she said, unable to lie either to him or herself any longer.

His eyes slid shut, and he sighed gently and slipped into oblivion.

Helen sat by Nick's bedside all that afternoon, waiting for him to come round after Theatre. Lawrence came, and told her that Mr Palmer was dead and that the police had arrested the son, and then he went, leaving her with Nick.

Finally, at about five o'clock, his eyes opened and he looked at her.

'You are here,' he said hoarsely. 'I thought I'd dreamt it.'

She shook her head. 'No, you didn't dream it, I am here.'

'Why?' he asked softly.

'Because I love you, and I'm a fool, and if you don't want me, just tell me to go away, but there's no way I'm leaving you unless you tell me to. Not now, not ever.'

His eyes were wary, the dawning hope in them quickly suppressed.

'I thought you didn't do relationships?'

'So did I, but that was before I met you. It's easy to make decisions about your future when you don't know what it might hold, but when someone offers you the moon and the stars, it's much harder to walk away, and I'm not strong enough. Whatever happened in the future couldn't hurt more than this, and I know you're not Tony, or anything like him. I have to trust you. I've got no choice. I'm nothing without you.'

She took his hand, drawing in a steadying breath, and forced herself to continue.

'On Saturday morning you asked me to marry you. Is the offer still open?'

He was silent for so long that her heart almost stopped, but then he smiled, a shaky, unsteady smile that he couldn't hold onto. He pressed his lips together and nodded. 'Oh, yes,' he said rawly. 'The offer's still open. There's no time limit on it.'

'Yes, there is,' she told him firmly. 'Just the moment you get out of that bed, we're getting married.'

His eyes closed, and when he opened them the joy he'd been suppressing shone clear. 'I love you,' he said softly, and she felt her control start to slip.

'I love you, too,' she said. 'I know you're sore, but—can I have a hug?'

He held out his good arm to her, and folded her firmly against his chest with a ragged sigh.

'I thought I'd lost you,' he whispered against her hair. 'I thought that was it, that it was over. I thought you'd leave, and sell the cottage, and my world was going to fall apart.'

'I'm sorry,' she said gently. 'I didn't want to hurt you, but I panicked. I didn't realise I meant so much to you—I didn't realise you meant so much to me. I thought there was still time to pull back, but there wasn't.'

'There was never time,' he said. 'We're meant to be together.' His hand stroked her back soothingly, and she lay with her head on his chest and listened to the steady beat of his heart that told her he was alive.

She didn't deserve to be so happy, she thought. He was right, they were meant to be together. She'd nearly lost him twice, but it was never going to happen again. She wasn't going to let him out of her sight.

There was a knock on the door, and she lifted her head to see Sam framed in the doorway, a couple in their sixties standing behind him, their hands on his shoulders.

'Dad?' he said warily, and Nick lifted his head and held his arms out to him.

Helen shifted out of the way as the boy flew across the room and landed on his chest. She saw Nick wince, but he said nothing, just clung to the boy with both arms and held him tight, rocking him gently.

'They said a man shot you,' Sam sobbed.

'He did. It's all right, though. I'm OK. He just got my shoulder.'

'Can I see the bullet wound?' he asked ghoulishly, sniffing and scrubbing his nose on his hand, and Nick laughed.

'Maybe later. It's lots of little ones, actually. It was a shotgun.'

Sam's eyes widened, clearly impressed. 'A sawn-off shotgun?'

Nick chuckled painfully. 'I don't think so. Just an ordinary one. I don't know, I didn't stop to ask.'

He looked past the boy to the couple hovering behind him, and dredged up a smile.

'Hi.'

'Never mind ''hi''. What do you think you're do-ing, getting yourself shot?' the woman asked, and turned her face into the man's shoulder with a little sob.

'Come on, Mum, I'm all right,' Nick said brac-ingly. He shifted himself up the bed a little with a grunt, and turned to Helen, holding out his hand to her. He drew her to his side and looked up at his parents.

'Mum, Dad, I want you to meet Helen Moore.'

They looked at her with interest. 'Sam's talked about you. You're the new doctor. You bought Mrs Smith's cottage, didn't you?' Nick's father said.

Helen nodded. 'Yes, I did.'

'And she's going to marry me,' Nick said firmly. 'Just as soon as I'm out of here.'

Sam sat bolt upright on the bed and stared at her. 'You are? Wicked! I'm going to have a mum again!' He stopped in mid-whoop and looked at her thought-fully. 'Are you going to make me eat vegetables?' he asked suspiciously, and Helen laughed.

'Not all the time,' she promised, and his face re-laxed into a smile again.

'Excellent. Can Tommy still come and play in the tree-house?'

'Of course.'

'Wicked.'

Nick's parents looked down at her and smiled. 'Welcome to the family,' they said warmly, and Nick squeezed her hand.

'Yes, welcome to the family,' he echoed.

Sam stood up and wrapped his skinny arms around her, and she felt a huge lump in her throat.

'Thank you,' she said softly. 'All of you.'

Her eyes met Nick's over Sam's head, and all the love he felt was written clearly across his face.

There was a tap on the door, and Lawrence came in, took one look at them and grinned.

'Thank God for that,' he said. 'I'll cancel the advert for another partner.'

Nick hugged her and Sam closer. 'You do that thing,' he advised. 'She's going nowhere. She's staying here with me.'

Nothing had ever sounded better.

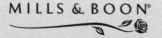

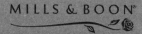

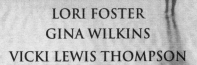

FREE

2 BOOKS
AND A SURPRISE GIFT!

We would like to take this opportunity to thank you for reading this Mills & Boon® book by offering you the chance to take TWO more specially selected titles from the Medical Romance™ series absolutely FREE! We're also making this offer to introduce you to the benefits of the Reader Service™—

- ★ FREE home delivery
- ★ FREE monthly Newsletter
- ★ FREE gifts and competitions
- ★ Exclusive Reader Service discount
- ★ Books available before they're in the shops

Accepting these FREE books and gift places you under no obligation to buy; you may cancel at any time, even after receiving your free shipment. Simply complete your details below and return the entire page to the address below. *You don't even need a stamp!*

YES! Please send me 2 free Medical Romance books and a surprise gift. I understand that unless you hear from me, I will receive 4 superb new titles every month for just £2.55 each, postage and packing free. I am under no obligation to purchase any books and may cancel my subscription at any time. The free books and gift will be mine to keep in any case.

M2ZEC

Ms/Mrs/Miss/Mr ....Initials ....
BLOCK CAPITALS PLEASE

Surname ....

Address ....

....

....Postcode ....

Send this whole page to:
UK: FREEPOST CN81, Croydon, CR9 3WZ
EIRE: PO Box 4546, Kilcock, County Kildare (stamp required)

Offer valid in UK and Eire only and not available to current Reader Service subscribers to this series. We reserve the right to refuse an application and applicants must be aged 18 years or over. Only one application per household. Terms and prices subject to change without notice. Offer expires 30th September 2002. As a result of this application, you may receive offers from other carefully selected companies. If you would prefer not to share in this opportunity please write to The Data Manager at the address above.

Mills & Boon® is a registered trademark owned by Harlequin Mills & Boon Limited.
Medical Romance™ is being used as a trademark.